He rested the butt plate of the Greener shotgun on one hip, covering the bar with it. "I need to ask you about a gent we found dead in the road a few miles south of here. Seemed like somebody shot him and robbed him and took his mule. Now, I hear tell you men rode into town leadin' a mule, so I was wondering if you could explain how you happened to come by that particular animal."

"Ain't no law against ownin' no mule," the redhead snarled, making a half-turn towards Slocum.

"You've touched upon the very reason I'm here," Slocum said evenly. "To find out if you really own that mule."

Another bearded man put down his shot glass and swung away from the bar, glaring at Slocum in dim light from a coal-oil lamp on the wall behind him. "Who the hell gave you the right to ask anybody any goddamn questions?" he said, as his right hand edged off the bar to be near his pistol.

The bartender, a plump fellow with a ruddy complexion, said, "You can't come in my place an' hold a scattergun on my payin' customers, mister."

"Like hell I can't," Slocum replied.

DON'T MISS THESE
ALL-ACTION WESTERN SERIES
FROM THE BERKLEY PUBLISHING GROUP

THE GUNSMITH by J. R. Roberts
Clint Adams was a legend among lawmen, outlaws, and ladies. They called him . . . the Gunsmith.

LONGARM by Tabor Evans
The popular long-running series about U.S. Deputy Marshal Long—his life, his loves, his fight for justice.

SLOCUM by Jake Logan
Today's longest-running action Western. John Slocum rides a deadly trail of hot blood and cold steel.

BUSHWACKERS by B. J. Lanagan
An all-new series by the creators of Longarm! The rousing adventures of the most brutal gang of cutthroats ever assembled—Quantrill's Raiders.

JAKE LOGAN

LOUISIANA LOVELY

JOVE BOOKS, NEW YORK

LOUISIANA LOVELY

A Jove Book / published by arrangement with
the author

PRINTING HISTORY
Jove edition / November 1997

The Putnam Berkley World Wide Web site address is
http://www.berkley.com

ISBN: 0-515-12176-2

A JOVE BOOK®
Jove Books are published by The Berkley Publishing Group,
a member of Penguin Putnam Inc.,
200 Madison Avenue, New York, New York, 10016.
JOVE and the "J"design are trademarks belonging to Jove Publications,
Inc.

PRINTED IN THE UNITED STATES OF AMERICA

10 9 8 7 6 5 4 3 2 1

LOUISIANA LOVELY

1

The newcomer had the look of a Missourian, Slocum guessed. Cold, calculating indifference to everything around him after what was called the war to end all wars. A look so common to men from Missouri who'd lost their souls, and some said all traces of a conscience, to bitter struggle and endless bloodshed.

Slocum knew men of his breed, for in many ways he was like them, although not a Missourian by birth, having only spent some time there after the war. But this was New Orleans, an odd place to find a Missouri pistol man, a gunfighter by trade—Slocum could judge the man's profession by the gunbelt he wore and his cautious nature when he entered the Delta Queen Saloon. He carried a Colt .44 with a five-inch barrel in a cutaway holster tied low on his right leg, and both the gun and holster had a seasoned look to them, showing signs of wear and frequent use, the application of oil to leather and gun metal, the mark of a man who depended on his equipment.

It was only a guess that this man hailed from Missouri, but over the years Slocum had become a pretty good judge of certain types of men, their origins, and most important of all, their profession when it involved the use of a gun. All too often his life had depended on knowing which man to watch closely when there was trouble brewing.

Slocum tossed back his brandy, keeping a cautious eye on the newcomer. There was an air about him, a confidence most men lacked, that made Slocum interested. But not wary. There were few men he'd encountered in his lifetime whom he'd feared, and they were only dangerous because they lacked good sense. A crazy man with a gun was among the most deadly, for he feared nothing, not even death, and while reason would cause rational men to consider the odds against them, a man without all his faculties wouldn't think about consequences. He would simply act.

Another type equally as dangerous was a coward. In Slocum's experience, more men died at the hands of back-shooters than from any other cause. Thus it paid to learn how to watch his backside as well as what lay in front of him.

He heard the stranger order a drink at the bar, and gave particular notice to the way the man watched everything in the room in a mirror behind the bar, eyes moving back and forth in the shadow of a low hat brim, a hat that had seen better days before rain and sweat and perhaps a trace of gun oil had darkened its crown and brim.

He's a careful bastard, Slocum thought, like a man on the run from the law, or from his enemies. So much caution was rare among saloon patrons, making him something of a curiosity. The Delta Queen was half empty, for it was early in the evening, and Slocum was enjoying himself over a few drinks after a long train ride down from Denver. A wire had come from an old friend asking him for help, and if there was one thing John Slocum valued more than beautiful women, it was a friend. It so happened that on this occasion, the request had come from both, a beautiful woman who was also his close friend, a friendship developed over many years. The telegram hadn't explained why Bonnie wanted him here in New Orleans—an explanation wasn't necessary. All Bonnie had had to do was say she needed him. He'd gotten on the first train out of Denver headed south. Four days later he was waiting for her here at the Delta Queen at the appointed hour he'd told her about in his answering telegram.

From the corner of his eye Slocum saw the stranger toss back his drink and order another, resting a worn boot on a brass rail beneath the bar. He was wearing dark tweed pants and a topcoat with patches on the elbows, the mark of a man down on his luck or the temporary victim of hard times. As before, his eyes continued to flicker back and forth across the mirror, watching everyone in the saloon.

He's on the lookout for somebody, Slocum thought, figuring it was most likely the law or a backshooter out to earn a bounty.

Slocum ordered another glass of imported brandy and took a Cuban cigar from his coat pocket. He'd dressed properly for the occasion in his best split-tail frock coat from a St. Louis haberdashery, paid for a boot shine, and put on a new paper shirt collar to go with a clean white shirt and string tie. His dress hat was an expensive beaver of the flat-brim variety, not the hat he wore while living out of a saddle. New Orleans was the sort of place where folks traveled in fancy canopied carriages and ate French food in the city's better eateries, not beans and bacon and cold biscuits or tortillas while sleeping on hard ground.

Slocum was accustomed to both ways of life. Good fortune had come his way in recent years and he could afford to stay at the very best hotels, drink good brandy, and smoke expensive cigars. Things had not always been like this, he remembered, striking a lucifer to his hand-rolled Cuban. Hard times had visited him on a number of occasions over his lifetime.

He blew smoke toward the ceiling, but with one eye on the Missourian at the bar. Slocum sensed something was about to take place, a meeting of some kind. Or a showdown between enemies.

In a moment of quiet he heard the bartender say, "What else for you, Mr. Younger?"

The stranger shook his head for a reply, and now Slocum knew he'd been right about the Missouri connection. The Youngers were blood relatives to the outlaws Jessie and Frank James, although he remembered hearing or reading somewhere that Cole Younger, the most infamous of the Younger brothers, had been killed or mortally wounded. If this was another of the Younger brothers, then why was he alone? Every member of the Younger gang was reputed to have a price on his head after the disastrous bank robbery at Northfield, Minnesota.

Slocum decided it didn't matter to him anyway—he wasn't in the bounty-hunting business. He'd made it a personal creed not to dig too deeply into other men's pasts. Hard times had pushed a lot of good men into making bad choices, and from what he'd read about the middle Missouri bunch, they'd had reason enough to go on a bloody rampage after the injustices forced upon them after the war.

A clock above the mirror told him it was almost time for Bonnie to arrive. He drank his third glass of brandy, puffing his cigar, counting the years since he'd seen Bonnie LaRue.

For reasons he'd never understood, she'd left city life in New Orleans to open a saloon and bawdy house in the farthest reaches of West Texas, a little hole-in-the-wall town named Dell City. It had become a hangout for tough characters and hardcases moving west toward New Mexico Territory and California.

But pretty little Miss Bonnie LaRue was no one to be trifled with. She could shoot as well as she could curl her hair or tie ribbons in her locks, and when a customer got too rowdy she simply gave him two choices . . . settle down or hit the road passing in front of her place. She called her establishment the Sheep Herder's Bar. And should anyone refuse either choice, she offered them a third option, the muzzle of a .36-caliber Colt she kept under her skirt. Those who didn't believe she knew how to use a gun soon discovered otherwise, and in later years a small cemetery behind the bar served as notice to all who came there that the proprietress could shoot straight, and often, if the need arose.

In her youth she was one of those rare women who had natural beauty, without the need for rouge or red lip paint or cosmetic help to attract the stares of men. But a marriage gone to ruin had left her with a bitterness from which she'd never recovered, and after a few years drifting from place to place, she'd gotten off a stagecoach in Dell City, Texas, with plans for her future and enough money to see them through.

It was several years later when Bonnie gave up the Sheep Herder's Bar to return to New Orleans and a quieter existence, to enjoy some of the finer things in life with the money she'd made in Dell City. And naturally enough, she'd opened another house of prostitution, a business she knew as well as any madam in the South.

Slocum still visited her from time to time. After all, they'd been more than friends. They became lovers not long after she moved to Dell City, meeting by accident when he rode through on the trail of a man wanted for murder and horse theft. Bonnie told him once that it had been love at first sight when he walked in her place, but with her lingering bitter feelings over any kind of relationship with a man, she could never completely give herself to him, and he, much like her, wasn't the kind to commit to a lasting relationship. So it was that with this understanding they became lasting friends and occasional lovers, and Slocum still valued her friendship as much as any he'd ever had.

A pair of French-style glass-paned doors opened inward and he saw her enter the Delta Queen, as did virtually every other man in the place. She wore a dark green velvet dress cut low in front to reveal the tops of her generous bosom, mounds of milky white skin spilling over the neckline of her dress, her breasts needlessly enhanced by the lift from a corset. Her gaze wandered briefly until she found Slocum seated at a corner table, which was his habit, keeping his back to the wall. She smiled and came toward him, the soft rustle of petticoats accompanying her to his table.

"John," she breathed, leaning over for a kiss, which also revealed even more of her cleavage as he was standing up to pull out her chair.

"You look so pretty tonight, Bonnie," he said, grinning when his gaze fell uncontrollably to her bosom, to the cleft between her luscious mountains of soft flesh. "If I didn't know such things are impossible, I'd say you've gotten younger."

She sat in the chair he drew back for her. "You always did have a way with words, John. And you have a way with a few other things. I'll warn you ahead of time I intend to get you in bed while you're here, so prepare yourself. I haven't made love to a real man in such a long time." She giggled softly as he slid back into his seat.

He admired her hair, done up in golden curls, and the

smooth ivory of her cheeks. He truly believed, looking at her now, that she'd gotten even prettier. He gave her a mock frown. "I've given up on women entirely, Bonnie. Can't find even one who can satisfy me since I left Dell City. There was a woman there who could buck harder than any bronc I ever rode, and she never did stop bucking until the sun came up. Unless I can find another woman like her, I'm finished with women forever. It's a waste of time looking for one who can take an all-night ride. They don't exist except in West Texas."

Her playful look stirred something deep within his groin, a memory of passion-filled nights spent with Bonnie.

"The same is true of men," she said. "They hop on and hop off before a woman can get warmed up. As you said, it's a waste of time...hardly worth taking off your clothes."

A saloon waitress arrived to take Bonnie's order.

"Give the lady a brandy, your very best imported variety, and likewise for me," he said.

"You remembered," said Bonnie. "How sweet of you, Mr. Slocum."

"I never forget a beautiful woman's wants or desires."

"And what if I said the only thing I desire is you?"

He chuckled. "I'd know instinctively you wanted something else. It would be your way of getting what you want from me."

"You wouldn't believe me? I'm disappointed." Her slow smile told him she was enjoying this game as much as he was.

"You know, I was disappointed when I learned you moved back here to New Orleans. I hardly ever get down this way."

"This is home. I was born here. To tell the truth, I got

tired of the heat and smelly cowboys in West Texas. I guess I was ready to live life a little easier.''

He looked at the Missourian standing at the bar when the girl brought them their drinks. The stranger was watching Bonnie in the mirror. Slocum's bellygun was hidden underneath his coat, and he wondered if the Missourian noticed a bulge where it hung in a holster below his arm. ''That gent at the bar is keeping an eye on you, Bonnie, looking at your reflection. You'll be able to tell as easily as I did that he's a shootist by profession or inclination, by the way he wears his pistol.''

Bonnie made a half turn toward the mirror as she brought her brandy snifter to her lips. Something she saw in the stranger's face made her hesitate before she took a swallow. ''That's Clay,'' she said quietly. ''Clay Younger. He's a part of the reason I asked you to come.'' She took a sip of brandy and turned back to Slocum before she added, ''He's a cousin to Bob and Cole, another hired gun from Clay County in Missouri. It's a long story.''

Slocum knew he'd been right about the man's origins. ''So start at the beginning. Tell me why a gunfighter from Missouri is in New Orleans, and what it has to do with you.''

''I'd rather tell you while we're in bed.''

''I wouldn't be listening. Tell me now, and then we'll give your mattress a try later tonight.''

Bonnie gazed thoughtfully out a nearby window at a lamplit street beyond the glass windowpane. ''A dear friend of mine has lost a daughter to a conniving son of a bitch who smuggles opium from the Orient. He pays top money to the right men who protect his illegal dealings. Clay Younger is one of his hired henchmen and by all accounts, Younger is dangerous.''

''How did the girl die?'' Slocum asked.

"That's just it," Bonnie whispered. "She isn't dead. She's only eighteen and that rotten bastard, Carl James, got her hooked on laudanum. He found her one day in a dress shop and offered to buy her anything she wanted. She was young and foolish. She accepted his offer. A week later she ran off with him to Baton Rouge. Her mother found three empty bottles of laudanum in her room after she left. When her mother and father tried to go to the police, they found out Mr. James has powerful friends in high places. They were told their daughter wasn't in Baton Rouge and no one was allowed to search the place. So because her mother is my special friend, I hired a couple of wharf characters who know their way around a gun and I sent them to Baton Rouge. They were both killed, their bodies found floating in a bayou. The girl is being held prisoner at James's plantation, and anyone who gets near her or asks any questions winds up dead. The police in Baton Rouge won't lift a finger to help because James is paying bribes to the right people to get his opium smuggled at night up the Mississippi."

"She's eighteen, Bonnie," Slocum protested. "In the eyes of the law she's old enough to make up her own mind about where she stays, or if she goes."

Bonnie gave him a cold stare. "You've never been addicted to laudanum or you'd know how wrong you are. He got her hooked, and now he won't let her leave. She's a good girl, not a saloon tramp, and she comes from a good family. I'll pay you whatever you ask, within reason, to go up to Baton Rouge and see if there is anything you can do to bring her back. I would consider it a personal favor, John."

Slocum watched Clay Younger's back a moment, finding their eyes locked on each other in the mirror. "Can't see no reason why I can't rent a carriage and drive to Baton

Rouge to see if I can find out anything for you. But I don't give guarantees.''

Bonnie smiled. ''The fact that you're here is guarantee enough for me, Mr. Slocum. Now, finish your brandy and let's find out if you're the man you used to be in bed.''

As Slocum and Bonnie were leaving the Delta Queen, he saw a man with a low-slung gunbelt heading for the French doors. He knew instinctively this was the man Clay Younger was waiting for, another gunman of Younger's ilk, probably a shootist who worked for James. He said nothing to Bonnie, having other priorities now.

Bonnie directed him to a polished two-seat surrey waiting in light from a gas lamp and parked beside a boardwalk running in front of the Delta Queen. A muscular man of obvious Creole descent sat in the driver's seat wearing a sleeveless vest. Slocum noticed an odd thing about the driver at once. His head was shaved, giving him a fierce countenance even though he wore no expression when he climbed down to help Bonnie into the carriage.

''This is Tomo,'' Bonnie said by way of introduction. ''He's my bodyguard, I guess you'd call it. At night, it isn't always safe for a woman to travel the streets of New Orleans alone. He is part Cherokee and part French—they call him a Creole—and he can handle himself if things get sticky.'' She took Tomo's arm and stepped into the rear seat of the surrey. ''He helps me keep things quiet at my place when a customer gets too rowdy. If you agree to drive up to Baton Rouge, I'm sending Tomo along to show you where James is keeping Josephine Dubois.''

Tomo gave Slocum a disinterested nod before he climbed back to the driver's seat.

''That's the girl you're looking for?'' he asked, taking his seat beside Bonnie. Slocum felt the big Creole would only get in the way, and there was something about him that made Slocum a bit uneasy. "I'm accustomed to working alone."

"You'd never find the plantation without him, and Tomo knows the back roads. You can trust him." She spoke to Tomo. "Take us home."

Without uttering a word, Tomo shook the reins above a team of black geldings and swung the surrey away from the Delta Queen at a brisk trot.

2

Slocum and Bonnie walked up wide steps leading to the front door as Tomo pulled the carriage around back. Faint light shone through etched glass windows from a spacious foyer. Manicured lawns surrounded Bonnie's two-story French-style mansion on Canal Street, and even in the dark Slocum could see it had once been home to someone with substantial wealth. But now, under Bonnie's ownership, the big house fulfilled another purpose, no longer a dwelling for a rich family as it had been in the past.

This section of New Orleans, called the French Quarter, had long since been given over to other pursuits. Some simply called it The District, and its present purpose was to offer gentlemen a selection of what was commonly known as the "sin trades." And if anyone in the French Quarter understood the business of trading in sin, it was Bonnie LaRue. She provided her clientele with the city's most beautiful women, in a setting so lavish that no one in New Orleans could rival it. The finest furniture seated her customers in a richly appointed drawing room. The best French wines and cognacs, Kentucky whiskeys, imported champagnes and liqueurs served in crystal goblets. Boxes of rum-soaked, hand-rolled cigars for gentlemen with the inclination. Amid all this finery, Miss LaRue rented flesh, some of Louisiana's most beautiful girls for a few moments or an hour in upstairs bedrooms. And Bonnie prospered because of her attention to the smallest detail.

"All my girls are probably still asleep," she said, guiding Slocum through twin glass-paned doors.

He took off his hat as a young girl came down a hallway.

"I'm back, Honey," Bonnie said, closing the doors behind her before the girl arrived. She turned to Slocum. "John, this is Honey." Then she spoke to the girl again. "This is Mr. John Slocum, a dear friend. He's here to help me find out what happened to Miss Josephine."

Honey gave him a polite bow. "It's a pleasure to meet you, Mr. Slocum. Miss Bonnie has spoken of you so often." The girl's face changed to a look that might have been fear. "We've been so worried about Josephine. That Mr. James is an awful man and I'm so afraid he'll harm her. And those ruffians who work for him are even worse. Miss Bonnie won't allow them inside here, and we're that much the better for it."

Slocum passed a glance up and down Honey's figure while she spoke. She wasn't his type, too slim-hipped and small-breasted to satisfy his cravings.

"The gumbo's almost ready, Miss Bonnie," Honey said. "Will you want two bowls sent up to your room?"

Slocum shook his head when Bonnie questioned his appetite with a look.

"None for me, thanks. I'm hungry for time alone with this woman," he said, giving Bonnie a wink.

Bonnie smiled. "You'll have to handle business tonight,

Honey. Mr. Slocum and I don't want to be disturbed. If anyone causes trouble, ask Tomo to take care of it. Make sure he puts on his coat and tie.''

"He hates those nice clothes you bought for him," Honey said, "and if you ask me it's like putting a silk dress on a pig. He's nothing but a big dumb Creole, and he's got a mean streak a mile wide when it comes to handling customers. He looks downright ridiculous in a silk coat and a necktie.''

The look Bonnie gave Honey silenced her. "I didn't ask what you thought of Tomo's appearance in a coat, Honey. Just be sure you remind him to put it on tonight. I'm sending him with Mr. Slocum tomorrow. Now, tell all the girls it's time to get dressed for the evening. It's past eight o'clock.''

"Yes, ma'am," Honey replied, backing out of the way as Bonnie took Slocum by the arm.

She led him to a broad staircase and showed him upstairs, to a room on the right of a second-floor hallway. Bonnie opened the door and swung it wide.

An oil lamp turned low on a nightstand beside a big four-poster bed revealed how truly successful Bonnie had been. Every piece of expensive furniture was waxed to a brilliant shine. He saw hand-carved dressers and wardrobes and bedposts. Dark velvet drapes covered high windows. A large desk sat near a fireplace. But the canopied bed dominated the room, its filmy netting hung like silken cobwebs above the mattress.

He recalled this room and its many pleasures from his last visit to New Orleans, but it was the woman who gave him the ecstasy he wanted and not a room full of lavish furnishings. He would have enjoyed bedding Bonnie LaRue in a haymow at the back of a livery stable, or just about anywhere else he could think of.

Bonnie closed her bedroom door, and Slocum pulled her into his arms, pressing his lips to her mouth until she gave a soft moan of pleasure. His hands ran down her back, searching for buttons that would free her luscious body from its green velvet prison.

"It's been a long time, Bonnie," he whispered, unfastening a button, then another.

"Too long, my darling John," she sighed.

He felt her dress slide from his fingers when she wriggled expertly, sending it to the floor in a pool of green material around her ankles.

"Can you handle corset strings?" she asked, giggling.

"I'll bite them in two with my teeth, if necessary."

His fingers found the laces binding her corset and he worked a bow loose. Her full figure almost exploded from the restraint of an undergarment she did not need.

"That's better," she murmured, sliding it down over breasts so large they quivered like mounds of egg custard with every move she made. Rosy nipples stood out, ends twisted, drawing his gaze downward momentarily.

"No prettier mountains anywhere in the West," he said.

She tugged the corset over her hips and let it fall to the rug.

He admired the gentle curve of her thighs, the rounding of her calves, and his hands went instinctively to her buttocks very gently, caressing them, kneading her flesh.

A gasp escaped her lips. Her eyes closed.

"That's the softest skin in the West," he added, his voice almost a whisper.

"Please hurry, John. It's been so long. Come to the bed with me now."

She removed one hand from her hips and led him over to the mattress, pulling back a quilted cover, revealing silk sheets the color of rose petals.

"Take me," she insisted, lying full length across the bed with her thighs parted. "I can't wait any longer. . . ."

He took off his coat, opened his pants, and kicked off his boots, stepping out of his trousers, tossing them on a bench at Bonnie's dressing table. Then he removed his shoulder holster and gun, and lastly his shirt and paper collar.

Bonnie was watching him intently. "You're still hard as a rock, John. I'm talking about your chest and arms."

An erection pulsed in his shorts until he slipped them off, revealing his throbbing member.

"Please hurry," Bonnie begged, placing a fingertip in the moist opening between her legs. "I feel like I'm about to explode."

"Then let's explode together," he said, kneeling on the bed to make his way between her creamy thighs.

"Several times," she moaned, rubbing her finger across her golden mound even faster.

He lay gently atop her chest, placing the tip of his prick against the lips of her hungry cunt. And then he kissed her very lightly, a teasing kiss.

Bonnie lifted her head off her pillow to stare down at his cock. "I'd forgotten how big it is," she breathed. "The first time you made love to me it really hurt. I was sore for two days after you rode off to New Mexico Territory."

"I'll put it in slowly," he promised, knowing she wouldn't want it that way.

"No!" she cried, reaching for his shaft, arching her spine to accept his offering. "Drive it in me, hard. I want to really *feel* it tonight. I want you to hurt me again, John. Please hurt me the way you did the first time. I want to remember what if was like to have your big cock driving deep inside me until I was sure I couldn't stand any more of it. And then I want you to give me more, all of it. Please!"

He pushed his cock between the lips of her cunt, feeling the heat of her desire and her wetness. Then he hesitated. "It's better if you take it an inch at a time."

Bonnie's head fell back on the pillow. "That's for silly little schoolgirls. I want it *all,* and I want it right now."

He thrust himself deeper inside her. She grasped his shoulders with her fingernails and moaned, rocking her head back and forth with her eyes tightly shut.

"Now, John. Now!"

He knew better than to oblige her completely, for his member was too large for her to accommodate all his length at once. He inched forward, and felt the muscles in her groin tighten with pleasure.

"Harder," she groaned, wincing, proof of the pain his big cock was causing inside her.

Slocum took her right nipple between his thumb and forefinger, pinching it, not too hard, but with enough pressure to bring her closer to a climax.

"Oh, John!"

He forced another inch of his prick into her, and as a reflex she dug her fingernails into his skin.

Her hips began to gyrate, quivering with desire and building passion. "Please, baby, give me more, and push harder this time, or I just know I'll die from wanting you."

He kissed her again, feeling her wetness moisten his balls and inner thighs. "You won't die, my darling Bonnie. You'll only want more."

"Then give me more!" she cried, thrusting her pelvis against him, still unable to take every inch of his thick shaft despite her desperate wish to have it all.

He began slowly, moving in and out of her mound, and when he did her breath started coming in short bursts, her teeth tightly clenched in ecstasy.

"Now, honey! Now!"

Slocum increased the rhythm of his thrusts and within just a few seconds, Bonnie stiffened and screamed, bowing her back as if she meant to rise off the bed and float through the air.

Minutes later his testicles emptied inside her with a wave of pure pleasure washing over him. He lay between her breasts, momentarily spent, looking forward to many more hours of Bonnie's insatiable desires.

3

A twisting road bedded with crushed rock and bits of shells
lay between New Orleans and Baton Rouge, a distance of
roughly seventy miles, Bonnie said, a difficult and oftimes
dangerous route passing beside the Mississippi River. She
warned the trip might take three days in a buggy because
of swampy roadways made worse by heavy freight wagon
traffic passing between New Orleans ports and Baton
Rouge, the capital city of Louisiana.

As Slocum drove out of New Orleans he passed Lake
Pontchartrain to the north, where small fishing vessels plied
back and forth dragging nets hung from long wooden
booms. Endless swamps, called bayous by local descen-
dants of early French settlers, stretched for miles to the west
and south. Clusters of towering cypress trees grew in the
swamps and on what little solid ground there was, spreading drooping limbs heavy with Spanish moss above creeks
and bayous. It was beautiful country, Slocum thought, very
different from his usual environs, and as an added plus,

southern Louisiana was full of truly beautiful women.

Yet the dangers Bonnie had warned him about kept him continually watchful as he drove a hired black buggy with a canvas canopy up along the Mississippi to find Josephine Dubois at the plantation of a smuggler named Carl James. Highwaymen and bandits were known to prey on unsuspecting travelers, for this part of Louisiana was still a relatively lawless place outside larger cities. Desperate men from the wharfs of New Orleans looking for easy pickings frequented the road to Baton Rouge, Bonnie had said, and by virtue of its being close to one of the most infamous towns for crime and violence, Natchez Under The Hill, some of the Mississippi's deadliest murderers and backshooters, many with prices on their heads elsewhere, were often lying in wait to waylay well-heeled citizens who had the appearance of being defenseless.

And by the cut of Slocum's attire now, as he traveled in an expensive suit and hat in a canopied carriage, he might appear to an inexperienced eye to be a perfect victim for a robbery. With a pistol hidden inside his coat, and both his sawed-off shotgun and rifle in the floorboard with his valise out of sight, he knew he might easily attract the attention of highwaymen, even with Tomo acting as an armed escort.

His bay buggy horse labored through watery wagon ruts a few miles northwest of New Orleans on a muggy day with overcast skies without passing any travelers, and he wondered if the early hour of his departure from Bonnie's might have something to do with the road's emptiness. Here and there, where the roadway passed close to the east bank of the Mississippi, he caught glimpses of heavy barges and flatboats moving upriver. Farther north he saw a giant paddlewheeler with thick black smoke rising from its smokestacks making its way steadily against a sluggish current. In places along the roadway he passed small houses, built on pole foundations to be aboveground when flood-waters rose.

While this was pretty country to visit, he knew he could never live here, not even at the behest of beautiful Bonnie LaRue. Slocum preferred open land, the West, mountains and clear-running streams and an empty horizon where a man could see range grasses for miles with no signs of civilization. He was at heart a loner, and while he often sought the company of pretty women and the finer things of city life, it was never long before he felt an urge, the itch to move on, to drift to another place he hadn't seen. He supposed it was the war that had changed him, making him wary of crowded spots and conformity—he'd had enough of that in the army. Having the freedom to mount a good horse and ride wherever he wanted was too important to him at this stage of his life, and nothing, not even the affections of a beautiful lady, would be enough to tie him down.

Tomo rode out in front of the buggy, as silent as ever, his clean-shaven skull glistening with sweat. His oversized arms and thick neck gave him an awkward appearance, but when he moved it was with a cat-like grace belying his bulk. He carried a twin-barrel shotgun sawed down to a murderously short twelve inches on a leather shoulder strap slung under his left arm. His skin was the color of creamed coffee, and while he did have some Indian facial features, it was also easy to see he also had some Negro ancestry. His chestnut gelding navigated the deepest ruts with an ease suggesting it was Louisiana-bred, though it did appear too small to carry a man of Tomo's size for any distance. Slocum hadn't wanted any company and he'd told Bonnie how he felt before they left, yet at her insistence Tomo came along anyway. It had long been Slocum's nature never to argue with pretty women when their minds were made up.

As they rounded a turn where the road crossed a narrow wood bridge over a bayou, Tomo halted his gelding and paid particular attention to a cypress grove east of the roadway. Slocum drove up beside him and halted his buggy horse.

"What's wrong?" he asked when Tomo offered no explanation for the delay.

"Someone be in them trees yonder," he said, his voice deep, thickened by a French accent. The sound of the Creole's speech reminded Slocum of a bullfrog's croak.

Slocum examined the trees where Tomo was pointing. "I don't see a thing, but if you figure we're in for a spot of trouble, I can handle it." He reached for his shotgun, a Greener ten-gauge with shortened barrels, checking both loads. "Wait here with the buggy and I'll take a look."

"Maybeso bad men," Tomo warned, still studying the trees and deep shadows underneath. "You stay. I go. Miss Bonnie say I be the one make sure nobody bother you."

Slocum left his buggy seat, balancing the shotgun in a palm after he climbed down. "I'm accustomed to taking care of my own problems, Tomo." He removed the hammer thong from his Colt .44 and walked to the front of the buggy. "I may look like a city boy to you the way I'm dressed, but don't let this fancy hat and coat fool you. Cover me while I slip along this ditch to see if anybody's waiting for us."

"I ain't supposed to let nobody shoot no gun at you, Mr. Slocum. Miss Bonnie have my hide if'n I do. You stay with dis buggy an' I go see who be in them trees."

"That just isn't my way, Tomo. I don't let anyone take chances for me. You stay and I'll walk the ditch. Bonnie will never have to know."

Tomo's flat face registered worry. "She done warned me you was gonna be dis way. But I give Miss Bonnie my word Tomo don't let you wind up dead like Pearlie an' Tibedeaux."

Slocum couldn't find any movement in the trees. "Maybe it's nothing. Tell me what you saw."

"Shadows," Tomo replied, as if it explained everything.

"What kind of shadows?" Slocum found it hard to believe the sighting of a shadow in the forest could cause so much concern.

"The shadows be men," Tomo said, and now Slocum understood. "No reason men be hidin' yonder 'less they be up to no good."

"Stay here," he said quietly, handing one buggy rein to the Creole. Resting the stock of his shotgun against his hip, he went off the road across a drainage ditch to a line of brush and small trees leading to the cypress thicket.

Fifty yards from the cypress grove he heard horses. Three men rode out of the trees, glancing in his direction before they turned north toward Baton Rouge.

"Tomo was right," Slocum muttered under his breath, watching the riders closely. They were bearded and poorly dressed and all of them carried pistols—one had a rifle booted to his saddle. A dose of caution on Tomo's part might have spared both him and Tomo a case of lead poisoning.

Slocum crossed the ditch and ambled back toward his buggy at a leisurely gait, resting his shotgun across a shoulder. "Looks like you were right, Tomo," he said when he reached the horses and buggy. "If I'm any judge of character by appearances, those boys had a surprise planned for us. When they saw me coming for 'em with a gun, they took off like they didn't want any part of us or these loads of buckshot."

Tomo was giving him a look of appraisal as he climbed back in the buggy seat.

"Miss Bonnie tol' me you was one tough gentleman with a gun, Mr. Slocum. She say you done killed a bunch of bad men when she knowed you in Texas. But dis here ain't Texas, an' you best be watchin' out for bad men who ain't inclined to show you where they's hidin'. They kill you afore you knows they's there."

Slocum shook the reins and sent the buggy lurching forward. "I'm acquainted with bushwhackers," he said, driving up beside Tomo in a pair of watery ruts as a light rain began to drift down from leaden skies. "I'm obliged for the warning you gave me back yonder, but don't worry youself all that much about keeping me alive. Men have been tryin' to kill me since I was mighty young, and nobody's gotten it done yet. I've got a few bullet scars and knife wounds to show for my trouble, but they were mostly all too far from my heart to kill me."

Tomo shook his head. "Miss Bonnie tol' me you was likely be the only man she knowed who could get Miss Josephine back. Dis bunch we's goin' to see in Baton Rouge won't take it kindly when we show up. Pearlie an' Tibedeaux was plumb mean to the core, an' they both winds up feedin' turtles an' gators. Dis won't be no place to act careless."

Slocum was watching the road ahead. "You'll find out I'm rarely ever a careless man, Tomo. I've made my share of mistakes from time to time, and nobody's got eyes in the back of his head. But I'm a pretty hard hombre to kill, if I do say so myself. You keep an eye on our backsides and we'll see if these boys in Baton Rouge are as tough as you say they are."

"They be plenty tough," Tomo replied. "We done seen plenty proof of that."

"What's this Carl James like?" Slocum asked, passing time more than anything else.

Tomo glanced up at the rain. In Slocum's opinion, it rained almost every day in southern Louisiana, another reason he could never settle here.

"He be a rich man," Tomo replied after a moment of thought. "He sell opium to the dens all up an' down dis Mississip'. Make plenty money. Calls hisself Monsieur James, only he ain' no part Frenchman of no kind. He come from back East someplace a long time ago, Miss Bonnie say. He got eyes like a snake, he does."

Slocum noticed a long Bowie knife sheathed on Tomo's belt, and wondered if he truly knew how to use it. "Best way to get rid of a snake is to cut its head off," Slocum said idly, as the cloudburst grew heavier, making the road harder to see for any distance in front of them.

As the morning lengthened, they encountered freight wagons returning empty to New Orleans, drawn by yokes of oxen or teams of mules. A few teamsters waved when Slocum and Tomo passed by, while others appeared to ignore them completely. And as the hour approached noon the rain slackened, becoming fine mist as the sun started to break through at times. Crossing wooden bridges over more and more bayous and stretches of swamp, they occasionally caught glimpses of the Mississippi off to their left where trees and undergrowth thinned. In spots, Slocum saw alligators sunning themselves on creek banks or floating on the surface, only their eyes and nostrils showing above the water, sometimes the ridges along their tails. Lower Louisiana was another world to a man from the West, and while it was beautiful in its own way, he felt no attraction to it.

With a suddenness that surprised Slocum, the skies darkened again and more rain came down, heavy drops pelting the canvas roof of his buggy. For half an hour there had been no wagon traffic or other travelers moving in either direction. Tomo unfastened a seaman's oilskin slicker with a pointed hood and covered himself from the thunderstorm. Rain filled every wagon rut, and now their horses labored through low places, slowing their pace to a crawl. Passing time, Slocum remembered last night and Bonnie's seemingly endless passion. Few women he'd ever known could be as demanding, or as tireless, in bed.

The crack of a gunshot startled him from his reverie and instinctively, he reached for his pistol. Tomo flipped open his oilskin and readied his shotgun, thumbing back both hammers before he reined his chestnut to a halt.

"Didn't sound like they were shooting at us, whoever it was," Slocum said, drawing rein on the bay.

"Come from round that bend," Tomo replied, pointing ahead with twin muzzles of his scattergun.

"Let's keep moving, only make it slow. If anybody takes a shot at us, head across this ditch. I'll leave the buggy an' hope my horse won't run off."

They advanced cautiously toward a turn in the road hidden by trees and swamp grass. What they found around the bend brought Slocum up short as Tomo stopped beside the buggy.

A man in a black broadcloth suit was lying in the middle of the road. A derby hat lay beside him. Three riders were moving north leading a mule with an empty saddle, galloping into a dark curtain of steady rainfall.

Slocum jumped down from his buggy seat, ignoring the rain, running to the downed man's side. Before he arrived he saw blood leaking into a watery wagon trace beneath the man's chest, and a dark bullet hole in the front of his coat.

A balding man with fleshy jowls stared up at him when Slocum knelt beside him.

"They . . . robbed . . . me," he gasped, blood trickling

from his mouth indicating the bullet had torn his lung. "I
... was ..." His eyelids batted shut and his chest stopped
moving.

"He be dead now," Tomo said, leaning over Slocum's
shoulder to peer down at the body from the shadow below
the hood of his slicker.

Slocum sighed and stood up. "Help me load him in the
back of the buggy," he said, glancing north where the three
highwaymen had ridden. "I figure it was the same three
bastards who were waiting for us earlier this morning.
We'll take the body to the next town and leave him with
an undertaker. I'll report what we saw to the town law and
give him the best descriptions I can, but the odds of getting
this poor fellow any justice look mighty damn slim."

Tomo's eyes had a curious light behind them, a smol-
dering rage he made no effort to disguise. "Dis poor man
don't even be carryin' no gun," he said quietly, but with
enough menace to make Slocum wonder what facing an
angry Creole like Tomo in a fight to the death would be
like.

4

It was a tiny settlement called Vacherie, a general merchandise store and an inn, a few houses built on wooden stilts, and a blacksmith's shop. Slocum drove his weary bay to the front of the store at mid-afternoon under the same rainy skies that had hovered over them since they'd left New Orleans. He climbed down from the buggy and sought shelter from the rain under a long porch running across the building as Tomo tied off his horse to an iron tether ring affixed to a porch post.

"I'll ask about an undertaker," Slocum said, taking note of several horses and a mule in a corral behind the store. While looking through the dead man's pockets he'd found a business card bearing the name Walter P. Simmons, and a notation that Simmons represented a firm in Memphis specializing in buttons and fasteners. Slocum walked inside the store, noticing the sweet smells of peppermint and licorice coming from candy jars atop a glass counter.

An elderly man in an apron came from the back, smiling

as if Slocum had been his only customer for quite a spell. "What can I do for you?" he asked.

"Got a dead man outside. Found him lying in the middle of the road a few miles south of here. A gunshot wound in his chest and empty pockets. I saw three gents ride away leadin' his mule. A card in the dead man's coat says he was Walter Simmons from Memphis."

The storekeeper's eyes wandered to a front window. "Three men rode up to the Willow Inn across the road a while back. They put their horses an' a mule in my livery. They said somethin' about havin' a few drinks. They looked like shady characters. But we got no law here in Vacherie. Too small to afford a salary for a peace officer. Next town of any size is White Castle, an' that's a day's drive in a buggy. You might mention what you seen to the law in White Castle. The city marshal's name is Gibeaux."

"What about the body?" Slocum asked.

"I get four dollars for a pine box, mister, but we ain't got no pauper's graveyard. The freighters charge two dollars to haul a coffin back to New Orleans."

"I'll pay the money," Slocum said, "if you'll notify his next of kin at the address on his business card in Memphis."

"How come you'd pay for buryin' a stranger?"

"Somebody has to. Can't just leave him lyin' in the middle of the road." He withdrew six silver dollars from his poke and laid it on the counter while looking through the same window at the travelers' inn across from the store. "You say three men rode up a while ago leading a mule?"

"That's right. They's over yonder at the Willow, only I ain't sayin' they's the ones who done that feller in. Just made mention of it, is all."

Slocum left the money and started for the door. "Thanks

for the information. Make sure you send a letter to that button firm in Memphis about Simmons.''

"You can leave the body down at the edge of my porch. I'll cover it with a tarp till I can get round to building him the coffin tonight, after I close.''

"I'm obliged,'' Slocum replied, walking outside. He made a motion for Tomo to carry the corpse to the end of the porch. Then he pulled the hammer thong off his hidden .44. "The storekeeper said three owlhoots rode up to that inn leading a mule. There's no law here in Vacherie, so I think I'll walk over and see what those boys have to say.''

"They be three of 'em, Mr. Slocum, an' you be jus' one.''

"I never was one to worry about the odds, Tomo. Just put the body over there and wait for me. If it's the same bunch, I aim to give 'em a chance to face a man carryin' iron. If there's one thing sticks in my craw, it's a yellow son of a bitch who'd shoot an unarmed man.'' He stepped off the porch and retrieved his shotgun from the floorboard of the buggy, making sure of the loads before he trudged across a muddy section of roadway to the Willow Inn, balancing his Greener in his left palm.

He entered with his usual caution, stepping away from the door frame as soon as he got inside, finding a lamplit drinking parlor thick with pipe tobacco smoke, a few empty tables, and three bearded men standing along a polished wooden bar, each one with a gunbelt around his waist. They watched him come in with no particular show of interest, until a short gent with a dark red mane of tangled, shoulder-length hair spotted Slocum's shotgun.

"Hold still, boys,'' Slocum warned, resting the butt plate of his Greener on one hip, covering the bar with it. "I need to ask you about a gent we found dead in the road a few miles south of here. Seems like somebody shot him and robbed him and took his mule. Now, I hear tell you men rode into town leadin' a mule, so I was wondering if you could explain how you happened to come by that particular animal.''

''Ain't no law against ownin' no mule,'' the redhead snarled, making a half turn toward Slocum.

''You've touched upon the very reason I'm here,'' Slocum said evenly, ''to find out if you really own that mule.''

Another bearded man put down his shot glass and swung away from the bar, glaring at Slocum in dim light from a coal-oil lamp on the wall behind him. ''Who the hell gave you the right to ask anybody any goddamn questions?'' he said as his right hand edged off the bar to be near his pistol.

The bartender, a plump fellow with a ruddy complexion, said, ''You can't come in my place an' hold a scattergun on my payin' customers, mister.''

''Like hell I can't,'' Slocum replied. ''I figure they're able to pay because they robbed that drummer and killed him. I saw these same three men riding away from the body, and one of 'em was leading a mule.''

''You're a lyin' son of a bitch,'' a black-bearded member of the trio remarked. ''You never saw us no place. Now I'm warnin' you to put down that goose gun. Appears you can't count, because there's three of us an' just one of you, an' by the look of that fancified suit, you ain't no shakes when it comes to shootin' an' my money says you'll run outta nerve facin' three men who know how to shoot. You're the same as dead 'less you lower that gun an' get the hell outta here.''

Slocum saw a motion behind the bar, and he swung his twin gun muzzles toward the barkeep. ''Don't reach under that bar for a gun, innkeeper, or it'll be the last thing you do. My advice to you is stay out of this if you aim to stay alive.''

"You ain't no lawman, so what's your stake in this?" another man at the bar demanded, holding his right hand near his holstered revolver.

"Just wanted to see if you boys had any backbone facing a man who's armed, that's all," Slocum answered. "I say you're all cowards, three yellow-bellied bastards who'll kill an old man who was defenseless."

"I ain't gonna take that kinda talk from nobody," the red-bearded man growled, hunkering down like he meant to reach for his pistol, his eyelids slitted with hatred.

Slocum grinned, a savage grin without mirth. "Go for it, Red. Grab that hunk of iron tied to your hip and I'll make your brains a part of the wall decorations behind you. My ol' Greener is a ten-gauge. It spits out enough lead to blow you in half, and your partners will be digging buck-shot out of their hides for quite a spell. I can't miss from here, being so close, so if you feel lucky today, then pull your piece and let's see which one of us walks away."

"You're an uppity asshole," another said, sliding his elbow off the bar very slowly to have his hand near his six-gun. "You wear high-dollar clothes an' come marchin' in here with a goose gun accusin' us of murder an' robbery without no evidence. Who made you the goddamn law round here anyway?"

"I don't represent the law," Slocum said, his grin fading to a thin line with his lips pressed together. "I represent a man by the name of Simmons who got robbed by three yellow bastards who bushwhacked him, just like you planned to do to me early this morning when you were waiting for me in those cypress trees. But you lost your courage when you saw me coming for you with this gun. Walter Simmons didn't have a gun, so you shot him off the back of his mule and took his money. In my book, that makes all three of you cowards and thieves, and I'm here to see accounts are squared.''

"I ain't takin' no more of this shit,'' the redhead said as he glanced to his companions. In the same instant he clawed for his pistol.

Slocum fired one shotgun barrel point-blank into the redhead's chest, feeling the shock of the explosion against his hip when the Greener thundered, slamming the stock against him with a force like the kick of a mule. The noise in the enclosed space was deafening, trapped by the inn's walls and ceiling. Flame and molten shot belched from the left-hand muzzle.

The red-bearded gunman was torn off his feet by the blast, lifted off the floor as though caught in a hurricane-force wind. He flew over the top of the bar with a strangled scream gurgling in his throat, tumbling backward, shredded bits of his soiled linen shirt swirling away from his body like tiny dancing dervishes. Crimson droplets splattered against the wall behind the bar as he toppled out of sight to the floor behind the counter where his drink sat, half full, his glass somehow surviving the hail of lead pellets.

Slocum was drawing his pistol from inside his coat when he fired his second shotgun chamber at the gunman with an untrimmed black beard. Midway through drawing his revolver, the robber's face seemed to disintegrate into a pulpy mass of blood and bone and tissue. Fragments of his skull erupted from the back of his head, attached to twisted plugs of matted black hair, flying through the air toward the inn's rear wall, the roar of Slocum's gun accompanied by a shriek of pain that ended abruptly when the man's cheeks were torn from his face. In the same fluid motion Slocum turned his .44 on the remaining gunman, who was frozen in mid-draw with his pistol, cowering backward, his eyes rounded with terror.

"Drop the gun!" Slocum snapped. "Or you'll join your friends in a cemetery!"

"Sweet Jesus!" the man cried, tossing his weapon to the floor with a dull thud. "Please don't kill me!"

The bartender suddenly threw up his hands, and that was when Slocum noticed a figure standing in the shadows of a doorway to a back room. Tomo was holding the barrels of his shotgun against the base of the barman's skull.

"Don't do stupid thing, go for gun," Tomo said quietly. "I kill you quick, *mon ami*. This be promise. You be one dead Cajun, you reach for you gun under dis bar."

The lone surviving gunman heard one of his companions groan while he was backing away from Slocum's Colt. "Don't shoot me. It was *their* idea to rob that ol' man, I swear by all the saints it was. Louie shot him an' took his money belt. You jus' gotta believe me. . . ."

The robber with his face torn to bits twisted and turned on the floor of the inn, moaning, lying in a spreading pool of his own blood.

"That's . . . Louie," the survivor stammered, pointing down with a trembling finger. "He done the killin'. I swear it."

Slocum addressed the bartender, who was also shaking with fear while feeling Tomo's shotgun touching the back of his head. "You saw what happened," Slocum said. "Two of 'em went for their guns first, so it was self-defense."

"You goaded 'em into it," the barkeep whispered. "You said they was yellow cowards. That's what you called 'em."

"And they were," Slocum explained, lowering his pistol to his side. "They shot and robbed an unarmed old man, a drummer who sold buttons and fasteners."

"You didn't have any proof," the barman continued,

with an eye on the redhead lying dead near his feet. "They were my cash customers, an' you killed 'em."

"It wasn't their cash," Slocum replied. "They stole it, and this is just what they deserved. I'll take the other one over to White Castle to the city marshal. He can tell his side, an' then face charges if the marshal's so inclined."

"I didn't do nothin'!" the gunman protested. "I was only ridin' along with Louie an' Rufe when they decided to rob somebody along the road."

"Tell it to the marshal," Slocum said. "Now move outside and saddle your horse. After you get saddled I'm gonna tie your hands, and if you try to run off, or do anything that don't suit me until we get all the way to White Castle, you've got my word I'll feed your brains to the sparrows."

Tomo moved silently around the bartender and took a revolver from a shelf below the bar. "I put dis gun outside, so you can find it after we's gone," he said.

The barman glanced over his counter. "What about this one? He needs a doctor, an' his face looks like beef hash. See how he's bleedin'?"

"I doubt if a doctor'll do him any good," Slocum answered, "but you can do whatever you want with him. I won't dirty my hands touching the murdering bastard. He got just what he had coming to him."

Tomo came around the bar with the bartender's pistol and the redhead's revolver, picking up the other two guns lying on the floor. "We toss dese in the bayou," he said to Slocum as they followed their prisoner outside.

"Suits the hell outta me," Slocum said, casting a glance at the store where the old man in the apron was watching from his front porch, drawn out by all the shooting. "We need to keep on the move as long as we can. I've got business in Baton Rouge."

5

It was dark by the time they reached Donaldsonville, a tiny village sitting on the banks of the Mississippi with several stores, a small clapboard hotel having just six rooms for hire, and an eatery advertising crawfish gumbo and corn fritters and fried catfish, served Cajun style. Tomo led their prisoner into Donaldsonville at a walk, followed closely by Slocum in the buggy under more of the same light rain. The prisoner, who only spoke once the entire afternoon, to admit his name was Andre, was soaked to the skin when they stopped in front of the hotel to inquire about rooms for the night.

In a small lobby lit by a single coal-oil lamp, a man in a pair of faded overalls stood behind a counter watching Slocum first, then Tomo, giving Andre only a passing glance.

"Good evening, *monsieurs*," he said, his gaze returning to Slocum's face.

"We'd like to hire a couple of rooms for the night and find a stable for our horses."

He frowned in Tomo's direction. "We got a policy. We don't let no Creoles stay here. It can be bad for business, you understand."

"Then I don't reckon we'll be needing the rooms after all," Slocum said.

"This here's the only hotel in town, *monsieur*."

Slocum turned for the door. "It wouldn't matter if this was the only hotel in Louisiana. I wouldn't stay unless my friend gets a room."

"I suppose I could make an exception."

"That's the only way you'll get my money, mister."

"The price is three dollars a night for each room. You pay in advance."

Slocum counted out six dollars, and while he did, the hotel man noticed Andre's hands were tied behind him.

"What's this man done?" he asked. "Are you a representative of the law?"

"He robbed an old man south of Vacherie. I'm taking him to the city marshal at White Castle."

"I didn't rob nobody," Andre muttered, and he was about to object further until he felt the muzzles of Tomo's shotgun touch his spine.

"Don't talk no more," Tomo warned, "or I's feedin' what's left of you to gators."

The hotel man handed Slocum two keys. "There's a barn in back where you can stable your animals."

"Much obliged," he said. "How's the food at that place down the street?"

"Best in Lou'sana. Hush puppies damn near float off'n your plate, an' crawfish gumbo . . . *mon Dieu!* The best."

Slocum touched his hat brim and walked out behind

Tomo and Andre, glancing over to the cafe bearing a sign above its roof that said "Claire's."

"We'll put these horses away and then get a bite to eat."

"How the hell am I gonna eat with my hands tied?" Andre said angrily.

Without a word, Tomo swung the barrels of his shotgun across the back of Andre's skull, making a cracking noise, sending Andre sprawling face-down in the mud road.

"He don't be so worried 'bout his hands now," Tomo said as he lifted Andre by the hair and began dragging him around one corner of the building unconscious.

"That wasn't quite what I had in mind," Slocum muttered, taking their horses' reins to follow Tomo toward a dark livery stable.

Delicious smells came from the kitchen at Claire's, but it wasn't the food capturing Slocum's attention at the moment. A dark-haired girl with pendulous breasts swaying gently beneath a loose-fitting white blouse was making him forget he hadn't eaten all day. She came over to the table where he and Tomo sat, with a smile on her face that would thaw ice off a frozen pond. She was pretty, a typical Cajun beauty with the darkest eyes Slocum had ever seen.

She ignored Tomo, staring at Slocum, still wearing her very best smile. "What is for you, *mon ami*?" she asked, her voice as sweet as her smile.

"I'll try the gumbo and hush puppies. The guy at the hotel said they were better than any in Louisiana."

"Are you staying at Le Frenchman's hotel tonight?" she asked, and the question surprised him.

"I am. Room number six."

Her brow knitted briefly. "You are not from this part of the country, are you?"

"I'm from out West. Colorado Territory mostly. I'm on

my way to Baton Rouge. I may be here for a while.''

A slight flush colored her cheeks. ''My name is Michelle,'' she said. ''If you come back later we have music, *le* Cajun music it is called.''

''My name's John Slocum, and I'd love to come back to hear a bit of Cajun music. Perhaps you can teach me to dance to it. I have never danced to a Cajun melody.''

''It would be my pleasure, Monsieur Slocum. The dance steps are very easy.''

''I'm looking forward to it. I'll buy a bottle of wine or a good cognac.''

''Cognac is my favorite, *monsieur*.''

''Please call me John. And bring my friend here something to eat, the gumbo and hush puppies.''

''*Oui*,'' she said, bowing slightly, hurrying off toward a door into the kitchen.''

''I suppose we oughta feed our prisoner something,'' Slocum said, remembering Andre. Tomo had tied him hand-and-foot inside the stable, binding him to a roof support with a buggy rein.

''I say we feed him to dem gators. He be too much trouble like he is.'' Tomo said it in a conversational way, almost like someone talking about the weather.

Two fiddles and a banjo kept time with a rub board and a Jew's harp in a small courtyard behind Claire's. Lanterns gave the dancers and musicians just enough light to see. Slocum held Michelle in his arms, following her footsteps in a combination of waltz and square dancing. After a few moments he was swinging her around to the music, and she was laughing. Between songs she drank cognac from a bottle he'd bought at a drinking parlor down the road past the hotel. Tomo had retired early, after checking on Andre's bindings, leaving Slocum alone to dance with the girl at Claire's.

"Are you a rich man?" she asked him between melodies, while a fiddler put resin on his bow.

"I wouldn't call myself rich. I live reasonably well, but I know what it's like to be poor."

She appeared to hesitate between swallows of cognac. "Are you a married man?"

He shook his head. "Never tried it. However, I do enjoy the company of a beautiful woman like you, Michelle."

"You have a devilish look about you," she told him, smiling coyly. "The way you stare at me, it is like you can see right through my clothing, making me feel naked."

"You have a beautiful body. You are truly one of the most beautiful women I've seen in Louisiana. I apologize if I stare too often. I can't help myself . . . I can't help wondering what you would look like without your dress, if I'm not being too bold or too forward by saying it."

"What you say to me makes my cheeks turn red," she whispered.

"You have very pretty cheeks. I suppose if I were a proper gentleman I wouldn't say such things."

Michelle moved closer to him. "If I were a proper lady I would not enjoy hearing them."

Slocum sensed opportunity. "After the music ends, perhaps you'll accompany me to my room so we can drink the rest of this fine cognac."

Her lips parted in another slow smile, revealing perfect rows of gleaming white teeth. "That really wouldn't be proper, would it?" she asked demurely.

"It would depend on several things, pretty lady . . . on whether or not you wanted to come."

"And if I said I *would* like to join you, what would you think of me?"

"I'd think you were a beautiful woman who wanted to spend some time with a man whose company she enjoyed, to drink cognac and get to know him better."

A fiddle began a squeaky tune, and the other instruments joined in.

"Dance with me, John," she told him softly. "Then we'll go to your room and finish your bottle. I won't promise you anything more."

Her soft cries of passion grew louder as his cock slid in and out of her wet cunt. Tiny drops of perspiration beaded on her forehead as the heat of her desire swelled. She gripped the edges of the mattress fiercely to keep from clawing the skin of his back to shreds.

"Oh, John!" she exclaimed. "Oh, dear sweet John!"

He thrust himself deeper inside her, bringing a gasp from the depths of her throat.

"No more," she protested weakly. "I can't take any more of you. . . ."

He rocked back and forth atop her, feeling her sweat-dampened breasts slide up and down his chest, nipples firm and erect, her skin so slippery he had difficulty remaining in position as he increased the tempo of his thrusts.

"It hurts," she murmured, clenching her teeth as though in terrible pain.

"Shall I stop?" he whispered in her ear.

"No. Please don't stop. Move faster, but don't make it go so deep."

Michelle began slamming her groin against his shaft in such a driving, pulsating rhythm he was forced to grab the headboard of the bed.

"John! John! I'm coming!" she gasped, clamping her arms around his neck, seizing fistfuls of his hair, grinding her soft hairy mound farther down on the shaft of his prick.

Suddenly every muscle in her body went rigid, and a rush of air from her lungs became a shriek of pleasure which she tried to contain by pursing her lips.

"Mon Dieu! Mon Dieu!"

At almost the same time he felt his balls rise, along with a sensation so intense he groaned. His prick exploded, sending hot wet come in irregular bursts into Michelle's cunt.

"Oh, baby," he hissed, clamping his jaw as tightly as he knew how to keep the sound from awakening everyone in the hotel while his testicles emptied.

A few seconds later she collapsed underneath him, panting for breath, her tiny nostrils flared, her mouth open, every inch of her body drenched with perspiration.

"Mon Dieu," she whispered one final time as her arms fell to the sweat-soaked bedsheet.

Slocum relaxed his grip on the headboard and lay gasping for air himself, locked between her rounded thighs while the last of his jism leaked into her cunt.

For a moment Michelle was silent, catching her breath.

He rose up on his elbows and kissed her lips gently. "That was one hell of a ride, pretty lady."

"You hurt me," she whimpered, tears forming in her eyes.

"I'm sorry," he said. "I didn't go as deep as I could have because you said it was hurting you. I tried to keep from it, only you kept pushing against my cock."

Despite her tears, she smiled a contented smile. "It's okay, John. It hurt, but in a wonderful way. I don't know what came over me. Do not apologize. I *wanted* you to hurt me."

He felt her juices mingled with his running down his balls. "I promise to be gentler next the time," he said.

She kissed the lobe of his ear. "Maybe I don't want you to be gentle."

"But you said. . . ."

She traced a fingertip along his cheek. "Pay no attention to what I say," she whispered.

"I'll never be able to figure women out," he told her with a grin.

"It is best not to try, *mon ami*. Most Cajun women usually want more from a man than he can give."

"You said you couldn't take any more, my darling. You told me I was hurting you, so I held back."

"In this case it was different. Never before in my life has any man been able to give me more than I wanted."

"You apparently never met the right man."

"I'm glad I met you tonight. Maybe it was the cognac that made me do something naughty like this."

"I wouldn't call it naughty," Slocum suggested. "Perhaps it was simply nice, the way it should be."

Her expression darkened. "I won't ever see you again, will I?"

"Depends," he said, thinking about what lay in store for him in Baton Rouge. The way he felt now, only a bullet or a knife would stop him from coming back to Donaldsonville to see Michelle again.

6

It had stopped raining during the night, and by morning the fog was so thick it was virtually impossible to see more than a few yards in any direction. Following a standing bath and a change of clothes, Slocum walked out of the hotel and found Tomo on a front step. Slocum's buggy horse was harnessed and the Creole's chestnut saddled.

"I go get dis Andre fellow an' tie him to his horse," Tomo said as Slocum loaded his valise, shotgun, and rifle into the buggy.

He'd been thinking about Michelle, and wasn't paying attention to what Tomo said. The girl had left two hours before dawn to climb through her bedroom window so her mother wouldn't know she'd spent the night elsewhere. "What was that, Tomo? I was remembering the woman."

"I get Andre," Tomo grunted, starting for the livery.

Slocum strolled along, casting glances at thick fog blanketing Donaldsonville. "Can't hardly see a damn thing in this soup this morning. Sure hope it burns off before too long or we'll be traveling blind."

Entering the stable, he watched Tomo bend down to untie the robber's hands from the barn post to put him on his horse. With little sleep last night, and the night before spent with Bonnie, Slocum felt groggy, only half awake.

The moment Andre's hands were free he sprang forward, wheeling around to make a grab for Tomo's shotgun dangling below his arm. Slocum reached for his .44.

The glint of a knife blade flashed in dim light coming from cracks in the stable wall—Tomo's reaction had been so quick it caught Slocum by surprise. The Creole's Bowie knife shot forward with lightning speed as the blade disappeared into Andre's belly.

Andre stiffened, caught in mid-reach for Tomo's shotgun with his fingers curling to grab it. Tomo drove ten inches of steel all the way to the hilt into Andre's stomach, and then, with the power only a man of tremendous strength possessed, sliced upward. The snap of bone and cartilage accompanied a yelp of surprise and pain when Andre felt the Bowie enter his belly, tearing through his rib cage. He staggered backward, and even then Tomo refused to withdraw his knife blade, ripping it higher inside Andre's chest. Blood squirted from a gaping hole in Andre's shirtfront, turning Tomo's right hand and forearm a dark red color. Only in the instant when Andre's knees began to sag was Tomo apparently satisfied. He jerked his knife free and stepped back to give Andre room to fall.

Andre sank to his knees clutching his belly, his eyes wide, rounded, blinking furiously.

It was, in Slocum's opinion, an inappropriate moment for Tomo to chuckle.

"Dis road pirate don't be botherin' nobody else now,"

he said, watching Andre's lifeblood flow down his groin, his thighs, pooling around his knees in bedding straw on the floor of the stable.

Slocum lowered his pistol. "I suppose we'll have to explain what happened to the authorities in White Castle," he said. "He was a fool to make a try for your gun like that."

"We don't got explain nothin'," Tomo replied as Andre rocked forward, landing on his chest, emitting a final groan. Tomo bent down, grabbing Andre's belt, lifting him as easily as if he were made of feathers.

"What are you aiming to do?" Slocum asked, watching Tomo carry Andre to the back of the barn, leaving a trail of blood on the straw.

"Feed him to dis swamp," the Creole replied. "Gators take care of him."

Tomo dragged Andre's lifeless corpse through a rear doorway, then to the edge of a bayou behind the corrals. Slocum holstered his Colt, figuring it was a rather crude but nonetheless very effective form of Louisiana justice.

Tomo swung Andre's body into the swamp with a quiet splash, kneeling down to wash blood off his knife and hand. A moment later Tomo returned to the livery, his face completely devoid of expression as though nothing had happened.

"We be ready to go now?" he asked.

"I reckon so," Slocum replied, giving the bayou a final look before he left the barn. "I'll have to hand it to you, Tomo, you seem mighty handy with that Bowie."

Tomo ambled through the stable doors. "Knife don't make no noise," was all he said.

Baton Rouge was one of the prettiest towns Slocum had ever seen, its streets lined with tall trees, tree limbs mantled with Spanish moss. Two huge wooden bridges crossed the Mississippi where the river ran past the city. Wagons and carriages and all manner of traffic crowded Baton Rouge's roads. Huge mansions, built before the war, rested in shady groves and on little knolls with manicured lawns and trimmed hedges. Magnolia blossoms gave the air a sweet smell, while flower gardens in full bloom decorated some of the better-cared-for homes. Tomo seemed to know where he was going as they entered the outskirts of the capital city, avoiding the center of town to take back streets leading toward a distant stretch of empty swampland to the west. As he led Slocum in the general direction of the swamp, they encountered fewer carriages and wagons. Farther west, Slocum saw a narrow road winding between thick forests of cypress surrounded by water. A sixth sense told him this road through the swamp would take them to the plantation of Monsieur Carl James, and a young girl he was holding a virtual prisoner with her addiction to opium.

He felt rested, after a good night's sleep in a hotel bed at White Castle. Tomo, while usually quiet, had told him things about his upbringing, a childhood spent in the swamplands of a place called Grand Chenier, then life on a riverboat plying the Mississippi to Memphis and St. Louis. He'd told stories of river pirates, and bloody battles over cargos of rum and whiskey in which he'd learned how to shoot and how to use a knife in hand-to-hand combat. And late last night, over a bottle of whiskey, he'd told Slocum about his meeting with Bonnie and how he came to be her trusted friend and bodyguard.

"We was unloadin' crates of rum from Jamaica on dis wharf in a bad part of town where don't no women go, 'less they's on the lookout for a man. There's more bad men in dis place than anywheres else in New Orleans. I

seen dis fancy carriage pull up to Fisherman's Palace, an'
I knows ain't no lady s'pose to be down on them docks at
night. A driver of dat carriage, he get down an' go inside.
I seen this pretty lady sittin' all alone an' I knows there's
gonna be trouble.

"Four men comes up to dat carriage, an' the lady, she
pull a gun. Only she don't see one dat's behind her carriage
with a gun hisself. I be gen'rally mindin' my own business,
but when I sees dat man with a gun I takes my blade out,
an' real quiet, I slips over behind. Dis bunch of men, they
be tellin' the lady she got to get down from her seat. She
say she gonna shoot any son-bitch who come close. Some,
they laugh at what she say like it don't mean nothin'.

"I come round behind real quiet an' slices open dat
man's throat, the one who got a gun. He don't make no
noise 'cause I got my other hand over his mouth. I picks
up his pistol an' come round to the side, an' say if don't
everybody get gone quick I shoot 'em all dead.

"One, he say he don't believe me. So I shoots him in
the leg, where it don't kill him 'less he bleeds too much.
Rest of 'em runs off like scared rabbits. Dat one I shoot,
he limp off fast as he can. Dat lady be Miss Bonnie, an'
she tell me if I come to her place on Canal Street, she give
me real good job so's I don't got to unload no more rum.
Dis be five year ago, an' I ain't touched no more crates of
rum or rode dat river no more."

Slocum was forced to admit he'd underestimated Tomo in
many ways, underestimated his loyalty and his toughness.
While he dealt out harsh punishment to those who challenged him, he was perhaps the best man Bonnie could
have working for her in a tough place like the French Quarter of New Orleans.

Tomo swung his chestnut around a corner and struck a

trot down the road heading into the swamp. Slocum found himself wondering what Carl James would be like. Most rich men had the money to hire protection, and from the looks of Clay Younger at the Delta Queen, James was making sure he hired the best guns he could find to protect his opium shipments, and himself. What Slocum didn't know now was how many gunslicks surrounded James and the girl, Josephine Dubois. Until he saw for himself, there was only guesswork as to the number of men he'd face trying to get Josephine away from Baton Rouge.

Dusk darkened the swamplands. Fireflies danced back and forth in shadows beneath towering cypress. Bullfrogs croaked ceaselessly, becoming a chorus with crickets Slocum could hear above the rattle of buggy wheels and the click of horseshoes on roadbeds of crushed shell. The swamp had its own smell, damp, slightly musty. Trotting his buggy horse down a single pair of ruts behind Tomo's gelding, Slocum wondered how far they would travel before they found the plantation. Mosquitos swarmed around his face despite the cigar he'd lit, hoping smoke would drive them away. As darkness settled over the bayous west of Baton Rouge, he began to ponder why he'd agreed to something like this. Of course, he knew why he'd come to Louisiana. Bonnie LaRue could have summoned him to Alaska—all she had to do was ask.

They traveled for miles without seeing a house or any sign of civilization, passing through endless swamp studded with tall cypress trees laden with moss. This wasn't Slocum's territory, and he knew it now. A man who hoped to survive in this wild land needed to know its secrets.

Tomo reined his horse to a halt suddenly.

"What is it?" Slocum asked.

"It be dat plantation belong to Mister James. You look close an' you see it from here."

He did see a faint row of lights burning on the far side of a cypress forest.

"Windows," he said softly.

"Dis be place where he keep Miss Josephine. Plenty bad men guard dis house at night. Maybeso we go on foot now, so don't hear us come."

"I ain't all that fond of alligators and snakes, Tomo."

"I keep eye out for gators. Snake don't want no troubles. Crawl away real quick, 'less you step on one."

Slocum slapped a mosquito feeding on his cheek. "I'll bring my shotgun," he said, climbing down from the buggy seat. "You just make damn sure we don't run across any alligators. I never did like big lizards with sharp teeth."

Tomo swung down from his saddle. "Gator, he don't want no part of a man 'less he's bleedin'. Even big gator don't figure he can make no meal outta us, if'n we don't get too close so's he get mad. We tie these horses an' walk real quiet. They's got a big gate blockin' dis road, so we's got no choice but to wade some of dis here swamp to get round it."

"That'll be like inviting an alligator to chew off our leg, won't it?"

"You leave gator to Tomo. Walk slow. Give gator plenty time get outta our way. Stay close behind me."

Slocum hadn't counted on wading through nests of alligators to find the girl. "Maybe we oughta come back tomorrow morning," he said, breaking open his shotgun, pocketing a few extra shells just in case.

"Come daylight they see us. Night, they don't s'pect nobody be out here."

Slocum wondered if he should be out in an alligator-infested swamp in the dark. He sighed, thinking of the number of times he'd risked his neck for the sake of a pretty woman.

Tomo walked softly along the rutted road for several dozen yards, then hesitated, cocking an ear as though he was listening to something.

"Did you hear anything?" Slocum whispered.

"Hear big gator squeak. Gator know we's here."

"Maybe we shouldn't wade through its territory. Let's find another way."

"Only one way," Tomo replied.

"Are you sure? Maybe nobody's guarding the gate."

"Dat be what Pearlie and Tibedeaux think. We go through swamp. Nobody see us there."

Slocum felt like saying the big alligators would know, but he held his tongue. He'd faced all kinds of men, desperate men who knew how to use guns and knives. But facing a giant alligator in a murky black swamp was another matter, and he could taste fear on the tip of his tongue.

Tomo edged off the road into knee-deep water thick with lily pads and swamp grasses, moving cautiously, pausing every now and then.

"We'll never see an alligator in time," Slocum said. "He'll be eating us before we know we're in the wrong spot."

Tomo did not answer him, continuing through deepening water a step at a time with his shotgun barrels resting on his shoulder.

He'd told Tomo all he wanted was to get a look at the place where the girl was being kept, to figure the easiest way to get close to her without shooting his way in. Slocum hadn't bargained on wading through alligators to reconnoiter the plantation, and the deeper they went into the swamp, the more certain he was that somehow, he would find a better method for getting inside Monsieur James's estate ... if he didn't become a meal for a gator before they got out of here tonight.

7

A feeling, a sensation when something underwater touched his leg, sent chills up his spine. Cattails and reeds and lily pads brushed against his thighs in the dark as he followed Tomo across a yawning expanse of shallow water toward a shoreline dense with underbrush and the inky shapes of cypress trunks. Until tonight Slocum would have said there was almost nothing he genuinely feared. But now, crossing a bayou Tomo said was full of alligators, he thought otherwise. Knowing this swamp was the habitat of giant reptiles with razor-like teeth and powerful jaws, he was forced to admit this was a notable addition to the short list of things he'd rather not tangle with.

"I can't see a damn thing," he whispered.

"A man gotta have cat's eyes in dis swamp," Tomo replied, making his observation while moving forward slowly, crossing a pool where water was almost waist-deep.

Slocum held his shotgun high to keep its loads from getting wet. His stovepipe boots were full of water, weighing down his legs. "I'd rather drive that rented buggy up to the gate and see if James's men are any good with a gun. I know what to expect if I'm facing a man, but I've got no experience with alligators."

"Gator ain't much different," Tomo said quietly, moving into a thick mass of lily pads. "Only gator ain't got no gun. Jus' teeth."

"I think I'd rather face a gun," Slocum offered, glancing over his shoulder to see if they were being followed by a pair of half-submerged eyes and nostrils with a long tail.

"Gator's got more sense than mos' men," Tomo said, working his way through a tangle of water plants. "Gator knows when to run an' when to fight. Some men ain't got no brain when they's carryin' a gun."

Something slithered past Slocum's right knee and he almost let out a yell. Whatever it was, he did not feel it again as they came nearer to the edge of the bayou whose solid ground had begun to look so inviting.

A high-pitched squeak, like that of a mouse, came from a dark spot at the base of a cypress tree.

"What the hell was that?" Slocum asked.

"Gator. He be sayin' not come no closer."

Slocum shivered despite the heat of summer. "Let's let him have all the room he wants," he said. "I'd rather face a dozen gunslingers I can see than one alligator in the dark."

Tomo said nothing, moving more slowly now, creeping up to the bank with greater caution than ever.

Slocum was happy to be in shallower water. Beyond the trees he could see lighted windows in a two-story mansion with columns across the front.

"That's one hell of a house," he whispered as Tomo inched up on dry land.

"Long time back it belong to rich man, name was Afton.

He own a hundred slaves. Raised sugarcane, folks say. When dat war over, he got nobody to cut his cane stalks. He done lose all his money without no nigras to cut cane, so he sell dis place to James.''

Slocum was still watchful for alligators even as they got to solid ground. His boots made a squishing sound when he took the first few steps into a cypress grove.

Tomo crept forward on the balls of his feet, making no noise until they reached the edge of the forest.

''Yonder be James's plantation,'' Tomo said. ''I 'spect we see plenty men watchin' dis house now. Flatboats come up bayou carryin' opium late at night. Pearlie say he hear tell they be real bad men, only he don't be scared. Now Pearlie be dead an' Miss Bonnie say she feel bad.''

Slocum peered through the trees. A building south of the mansion caught his attention. ''That looks like a canal running up to a shed of some kind.''

''Be boathouse,'' Tomo whispered. ''Flatboat bring load of opium up dis canal. Men unloads it quick, Tibedeaux say. He know dis flatboat cap'n who bring it here. Tibedeaux tell Miss Bonnie he can get Miss Josephine back easy, if she pay him an' Pearlie five hundred dollar. She pay half, only Pearlie an' Tibedeaux don't come back 'cause they be dead.''

The front porch across the house, supported by massive white columns, appeared deserted. ''I don't see anybody moving around. No guards. Nothing.''

''They's here,'' Tomo replied, as if he was sure of it.

Tomo moved silently among the cypress trunks, edging toward the boathouse, keeping to the deepest shadows. Slocum crept forward as quietly as he could with boots full of water, keeping an eye out for alligators, and for gunmen in the trees surrounding the plantation. While lamps were lit behind windows of the main house, he saw nothing—no one moving, no shadows that might have been men standing guard anywhere near the mansion or boathouse. It was as if the place had been deserted.

Tomo halted suddenly, pointing to the canal. "Man be near dis tree," he whispered. "He stand still so we don't see him in dark."

Slocum's eyes slitted. "I see a shape. I suppose it could be a man."

"Be lookout," Tomo replied.

"You're eyes are better than mine."

"Take practice, see in dark. Look for outline. Tree no have shape like dis."

A form stood out among forest shadows, an outline standing near the trunk of a thick cypress tree.

"I see him now," Slocum said softly.

A movement near the boathouse caught Slocum's eye. A man with a rifle walked out on a narrow wharf, looking up and down the canal.

"There's another one," Slocum whispered. "He's looking across the bayou like he's expecting something . . . or someone."

"Flatboat come," Tomo said. "Maybeso soon. We wait here. See how many men come when flatboat comes."

"These mosquitos are about to eat me alive," Slocum protested, waving a hand in front of his face.

"Be better if *bug* draw blood," Tomo answered. "Bullet come, we no get out of dis place alive."

Content to watch from the darkness for now, Slocum gave some thought to how he'd try to rescue the girl. Only one road led in and out of the plantation. Escaping on horseback, or in a buggy, was the only logical way to get her away from this place. While he'd never met Josephine Dubois, he felt sure no woman would wade across this alligator-infested swamp.

A dim light appeared in the distance, coming up the canal. Slocum watched it for a moment, watched its movement. "Here comes the boat," he told Tomo.

Tomo nodded his silent agreement.

"The road, or that canal, is the only way in or out of here by the look of things," Slocum said. "If we aim to get the girl out alive, it'll have to be by boat, or riding hell-for-leather down that road."

"Be plenty guns shootin' either way," Tomo replied in a voice so quiet Slocum had trouble hearing him.

"If James has paid shootists like Clay Younger on his payroll, they'll be good shots," Slocum added.

"Worst one be Joe Wales," Tomo said. "He be meanest of all dem shooters. Joe Wales don't be scared of nobody, an' I hear folks say he shoot good. Real good."

Slocum knew he'd heard that name before. "Joe Wales rings a bell. I've heard of him."

"He take money from who got the most of it. Creole medicine woman say he got nine lives, like a cat. She say voodoo spell no work on Joe Wales, 'cause he got no soul."

Slocum knew little or nothing about voodoo superstition, and he said, "I never was one to put much stock in magic spells or things like that. A bullet in the right spot works better'n any magic I ever heard of."

Tomo grunted. "You never see dead man walk. Bullet don't do no good when man already dead."

"I don't believe in that sort of thing. Dead men don't walk around."

"Tomo see. Rise up from grave at night when voodoo spell say it be time," Tomo whispered.

It was pointless to argue against Tomo's beliefs, and Slocum let it drop to watch the canal. A small flatboat with a lantern hanging from a boom at the front of the craft came slowly up the canal, poled by three men, one on each side and one standing at the rear.

And now men began coming out on the wharf, men carrying guns of every description, rifles and shotguns and pistols. Slocum counted six, and there was the lookout posted beside the cypress tree not far away.

"James has got himself a regular army," Slocum observed in a hushed voice.

"There be one or two more keep eye on gate," Tomo replied, turning his head as though he was listening for something.

"What is it?" Slocum whispered, taking his own cautious look at the swamp behind them.

"Gator move. Go in water. Maybeso get away from somebody who come up behind us."

"I didn't hear anything."

"Mos' white men don't know bayou sounds. Creole learn to listen good when he a baby. If he don't, he no grow up to be man."

No matter how hard Slocum looked, he saw nothing in the forest around them, and there were no noises other than a constant chorus of bullfrog croaks and crickets chirping. In the dark it was impossible to see anything in detail other than the wink of fireflies.

He watched the boat draw closer to the wharf, and still saw only six armed men awaiting its arrival. While these weren't the kind of odds he favored, he'd been in more lopsided fights before and managed to come out of them alive.

"I've seen enough," Slocum whispered. "Only two ways in or out, the road or by boat. The only way to get the lay of things inside that house is to try to get an invitation. If I pose as a buyer for some of his opium, maybe I can drive right through the gate."

"They no let you bring gun," Tomo said, continuing to gaze over his shoulder at the swamp.

"Then I'll hide one here tonight as close to the house as we can get without being seen. If James buys my story that I'm interested in purchasing raw opium from him, he might relax his guard just long enough for me to walk the grounds. I'll pick up the gun I've hidden and make my move to get the girl, if I think it stands a chance of working. If I can find a place to hide my bellygun in the fork of a tree someplace . . ."

Tomo appraised him with a sideways look. "Jus' one gun?" he asked.

Slocum studied the grounds around the mansion again. "It may be the only way I can pull it off, and I'll be gambling I can get to it without getting shot in the back or having any harm come to Josephine. Bonnie would never forgive me if anything happens to the girl."

Tomo wagged his head. "You either be brave man, or crazy like loon bird."

Slocum thought about it. "Probably a little of both. Now let's find the fork of a tree I'll recognize where I can hide my pistol. If James won't invite me out to talk business with him, the most I will have lost is a forty-dollar gun."

Tomo gave the clearing around the house a thorough examination. Then he beckoned for Slocum to follow him, edging away from the spot where they'd been watching the flatboat arrive. Slocum did his best to keep his wet boots from making noise as they crept through the forest. Somehow, even though Tomo had waded across the same swamp, his feet made no discernible sound as they drew closer to the edge of a lawn where the cypress trees had been cleared away.

Tomo led him to a tree with a fork in the trunk roughly six feet from the ground. There, Slocum left his bellygun, and as an afterthought, he placed his short-barreled Greener atop a thick limb, along with two extra shells, leaving him for the moment without a weapon. He hated to part with either gun, and there was a chance he'd never be able to retrieve them if his plan to get an invitation to the James plantation failed. But with the safety of Josephine Dubois in mind, it was out of the question to think he and Tomo could shoot their way in and get her out alive. Subterfuge seemed like a more workable idea, if anything stood a chance of getting the job done.

"Let's go," he whispered to Tomo, glancing toward the boathouse, where men carried small crates from the flatboat up the wharf.

Tomo gave him another questioning look, then nodded and moved quietly away from the clearing. Slocum was only guessing, but he figured that Tomo thought he was completely crazy and didn't approve of the idea of leaving hidden guns here. While Tomo was clever in his own way, clearly knowledgeable in the ways of bayous and swamps and alligators and Louisiana cutthroats, he appeared to have little experience with more subtle methods when it came to dealing with lawless men. Slocum was counting on the most powerful weapon of all, greed, to get him inside the plantation. Greed might entice Monsieur Carl James to let his guard down.

8

The Grand Lenier Hotel in Baton Rouge suited his tastes. A tile bath at the end of a second-floor hallway offered a cast-iron tub filled with hot water and scented soap while he rested and smoked a rum-soaked cheroot, sipping brandy from a bottle he'd had sent up from the bar downstairs. Mosquito bites covered his face and hands, and when he'd rented his room the hotel clerk had given him a suspicious look until she saw the gleam of his money. His pants and boots had smelled too much like swamp water when he strode into the lobby, after putting his horse and buggy at a livery down the street. Tomo had said he knew a young Creole woman in Baton Rouge he wanted to see that night, leaving Slocum to the Grand Lenier by himself.

A mulatto girl brought him more buckets of hot water from time to time. Her skin was so fair it resembled the yellow butter Slocum's mother used to churn, and her eyes were a deep shade of green. She wouldn't look at his nakedness when she entered the bath, eyes averted while she slowly poured more steaming water into his tub.

"What's your name?" he asked on her third trip upstairs with buckets.

She batted long eyelashes. "Claudette," she replied, even more embarrassed when he spoke to her so directly.

"It's a pretty name. French, isn't it?"

"I've got some French blood, my mammy says. Most everybody in Louisiana do got some in 'em. Folks call us quadroons."

"My name's John."

"Very pleased to meet you," she said with a polite bow.

"You look young. I'd guess sixteen."

"I'm older," she answered. "Almost twenty."

She was wearing a shapeless, faded cotton dress that had lost its color from too many washings.

"I couldn't see your figure, I reckon, and that's why I guessed wrong. That dress you're wearing hides a woman's shape and I couldn't tell you were older."

"I haven't got many dresses," she said. "We're poor folks an' dresses are expensive. My mammy made this one for me a long time ago."

He looked more closely at the swell of her bosom. "A real pretty lady shouldn't hide her charms. Men like to look at the figure of an attractive woman now and then."

Her smile was one of deeper embarrassment. "You say the sweetest things, makin' me feel pretty even if this ol' dress covers me up. Thank you, sir, for sayin' it."

"How much does a dress cost in Baton Rouge? A really nice one?"

"More money'n there is in the whole world, maybe much as ten or fifteen whole dollars. A piece of a bolt of cloth don't cost all that much. A dollar or two."

"A young man who wants a beautiful woman would pay ten or fifteen dollars to buy you a dress, wouldn't he?"

She shook her head. "No, sir. The menfolks I know is all as poor as church mice, like we are."

He stirred in the soapy water, leaning his head back against the tub to further admire her beauty. "Silk stockings too. You need a pair of silk stockings to go with a new dress."

She put down her buckets. "Those things are jus' dreams for a poor girl," she said. "Silk stockings are for rich folks."

He chuckled over her continuing bashfulness. "A woman's real beauty lies underneath. It's not what she's wearing, but what she's covering up with dresses and stockings, that catches a man's eye."

Claudette giggled. "You're makin' my face feel hot. Wish you wouldn't say all them things."

"I'm only being honest, Claudette. Underneath that dress is a beautiful lady, only no one will ever know what's under there unless you take it off or wear dresses that show your figure."

"Can't afford no new dress," she said, looking down at the floor.

"You seem very bashful, and yet you have no reason to be. I know a pretty woman when I see one. You should learn to take a compliment when it's sincere."

"Nobody ever says that kind of thing to me," she told him, unable to look him in the eye.

He blew smoke toward the ceiling. "I'm saying it now. And I mean every word of it. You're very pretty. A woman with a full figure should show it off to her best advantage by wearing clothes flattering her shape. I'm quite sure that underneath your homemade dress there's a striking figure."

She smoothed the front of her skirt. "You're jus' sayin' that, hopin' I'll show you."

Slocum glanced at his pocket watch on a dressing table

next to the tub. It was past two o'clock in the morning. "I'd call it an honor to catch a glimpse of such a beautiful woman without her clothes, but I wouldn't expect you to do it unless you wanted to."

"I do believe you're jus' funnin' with me," she said as a trace of color rose in her cheeks.

He stubbed out his cigar in a nearby ashtray and stood up slowly, water and soap suds dripping down his hairy chest, his pubic hair, his prick and balls. "I'm not playing games with you, Claudette," he told her gently. "I think you are a remarkably beautiful woman."

At first, she looked away quickly, until her eyes strayed back to his cock briefly. "You sure are . . . big, Mr. John. I don't b'lieve I ever did see one so big as that. Course, I ain't seen all that many either."

He reached for a towel and stepped out of the tub, standing very close to her as he dried himself off. "Some women say it feels good inside 'em." He patted his balls and prick dry very carefully. All the while, Claudette was staring down at his thickening member—it was her stare, and what it foretold, that gave rise to a slow swelling in his cock.

"Looks like it would hurt," she said, her voice barely above a whisper.

"Like anything else, from a bullwhip to a gun, it depends on how it's used. Why don't you come down the hall to my room and I'll show you how it can be used very gently. We can share the rest of this bottle of brandy."

She took a half step backward, still watching his cock with a look of fascination. "I might get in trouble with Miz Lenier if I did that," she replied.

"It's after two. Nobody's gonna want any bathwater brought up at this hour."

"Maybe she's done gone to bed by now," Claudette said with a glance over her shoulder at the bathroom door. "I s'pose I could go down real quiet an' see." Her gaze returned to his prick. "It ain't very lady-like to say so, but I sure would like to know what . . . that thing feels like."

"I'm in room twenty-five down the hall," he said, letting his towel fall to the floor. "I'll leave the door unlocked so you can come in whenever you wish."

"I hadn't oughta," she told him. "It'd be wrong to jus' be jumpin' in a bed with a strange man I don't hardly know at all."

"No one but the two of us will ever have to know," he said, giving her a one-sided grin.

"I'll go down an' see if Miz Lenier is asleep, if she's done hung up the Closed sign in the front door."

He watched Claudette hurry out of the bath with her buckets as he gathered up his clothes. "Damned if these Louisiana women aren't all pretty," he muttered, tiptoeing down a carpeted hall to reach his room with the bottle of brandy clenched in his left fist.

He heard a gentle tapping on his door as he lay naked with his face to an open window, enjoying the cooler air of night.

"Come in," he said softly, lowering the wick on an oil lamp on a bedside table so that the room was almost totally dark.

Claudette came in and closed the door behind her. She saw him reposing on the four-poster bed with his heavy cock resting against his thigh.

She crossed over to the bed and stared down at his prick for a moment. "Lordy, but that thing do look large," she whispered.

He grinned, propping his head up on both feather pillows. "Now you can take off that dress so I can see how right I was about your figure."

"It'd be better if you turned out the lamp," she protested in a quiet voice.

"But then it would be too dark for me to see if I was right about things," he responded. "Don't be so bashful. You have no reason to be ashamed of what you look like without any clothes."

She began unbuttoning her top buttons, stepping out of her worn sandals while she continued to open the front of her dress. "Don't pay me no mind if I act a little nervous," she said. "I never did do this before, not with a man I jus' met about an hour ago."

"I'll help you get rid of your nervousness," he said. "Come over here and I'll help relax you."

Claudette wriggled out of her dress. It fell around her ankles, revealing she was completely naked underneath. She had bulbous breasts the size of ripe melons, a creamy color in the half-dark accented by dark red nipples. A tiny mound of curled pubic hair grew at the tops of her thighs.

"Come here," he whispered throatily, just as his prick began to rise, becoming engorged with blood at the sight of Claudette's magnificent body.

She took a few tentative steps toward the mattress, until he reached for her hand.

"Touch this," he said, wrapping her thin fingers around his stiffening cock. "You see? It won't bite you."

She giggled softly, then bent down to give it a closer inspection. She stroked his shaft gently a few times, until she let out a deep sigh and opened her mouth.

She took the head of his cock between her lips, only the tip at first, running her tongue over it, licking his foreskin and the underside of his glans.

He let out a helpless moan, feeling warmth spread through his groin, beginning in his balls.

Claudette started making sucking sounds as her head

bobbed up and down, her mouth taking his cock deeper and deeper with each thrust. His hip muscles tightened with the ecstasy of an intensifying pleasure. His testicles rose higher.

He watched the sway of her breasts as the tempo of her head movements increased. Reaching for one dark nipple, he squeezed it between his thumb and forefinger, rolling it back and forth until it grew hard, twisted.

"Oh, that feels good, Claudette," he groaned. It felt as if his balls were about to explode. His prick throbbed, sending a wave of sensation all the way to his toes each time her tongue passed over his glans.

She gripped the base of his shaft, and he noticed her hand trembling with desire. The sucking sounds she made grew louder and louder.

"Climb on top of me," he sighed. "I can't take much more of this or I'll bust wide open."

She took his cock from her mouth and knelt on the edge of the bed, swinging one beautiful curved thigh over him. Placing her hairy mound over the tip of his prick, she pulled the lips of her cunt apart and lowered herself onto a few inches of his shaft until she felt too much resistance.

"It won't fit," she gasped, panting now, making very short thrusts downward until she could go no further.

"Give it time," he whispered, gripping her slender waist with both palms, rocking gently upward to meet her thrusts.

"It jus' ain't gonna go," she said, thrusting faster, yet allowing his cock to go no deeper. Beads of sweat formed on her brow and between her heavy breasts, glistening in light from the lamp.

"It'll go in a moment or two, baby," he told her, rising a bit higher inside her wet cunt despite a very tight fit. "Give me time to help you relax. Let yourself go."

"I want it inside me real bad," she moaned, her eyes closed as though she was in pain, or the throes of a passion so intense it forced her to continue in spite of the hurt.

His balls were about to burst from her warmth and the damp slickness surrounding his cock. While he didn't want to cause her any real pain, he found he was helpless to control his deepening thrusts.

She was panting so hard now he could hear her breath whispering through her nostrils and lips.

"Deeper!" she cried suddenly as she started hammering her pelvis down on his shaft with tremendous force, the noise from her wetness like that of a water-soaked fireplace bellows.

He rose upward powerfully, feeling her cunt resist his deep penetration, and she pushed herself down further, taking all of it inside her.

"Oh, God," she screamed as the tip of his member reached into the deepest recesses of her cunt. Pounding against places that had never been touched before. Finding a trigger point that would send her over the edge.

"I can't hold back any longer," Slocum panted as he shot cum into her. He felt her begin to contract around his member, and knew that she had reached her pinnacle with him. The rhythmic contractions were slowing milking him for all he was worth, and he felt she was going to drain him of all that he had. The tightness of her caused him sweet pain as she collapsed on his chest in one final cry of passion.

As their breathing slowed, Slocum could tell she was still aroused.

"John, you're still hard. Didn't you get enough?"

The stiffness inside her prompted her to start grinding her pelvis against him again. He could feel the throbbing of her mound around his member, and the rising of his balls to meet the demand her cunt was placing on him to fire his jism again. He rolled her over on her back and plunged himself inside her, holding back not one inch of his substantial length.

"Yes, John. Go deeper, give me more of it. Fill me up with it."

Slocum knew she would be sore in the morning, but he could no longer contain himself. When the milking started again, he knew he was a goner. He shot his second load of seed inside her as her nails clawed at his back. Her legs wrapped around his waist, locking him to her body, imprisoned in her cunt.

9

"His name be Ledeaux," Tomo said, as they stood in on the banks of the Mississippi shortly after noon. "He be the one who get you introduction to Monsieur James. Ledeaux run dis dice game at a place called the Palace. You ask for Ledeaux, an' if don't nobody think you be police, Ledeaux come talk to you. It be dangerous place, the Palace. Don't leave no room 'tween you an' no walls or you liable feel taste of knife blade."

"It's down by the boat docks?" Slocum asked.

"I take you there. Wait outside. If there be trouble, I come quick."

Slocum was wearing his Colt .44 in a cross-pull holster hidden underneath his frock coat. He'd strapped his little .32-caliber derringer inside his left boot, just in case. Other than his Winchester rifle, he was down to the last of his weaponry after leaving his bellygun and Greener in the fork of a tree at the James plantation.

"I can handle myself, Tomo," he said, watching a huge

barge being pulled upriver by a steam-driven tugboat. "No need for you to wait outside the Palace."

"Miss Bonnie say I watch out for you."

"Bonnie ought to know by now I don't need anyone watching my back. But if you insist, you can show me the way to the Palace and then wait outside."

"Be Miss Bonnie's orders," Tomo said, turning away from the river.

In truth, Slocum felt a little better having the big Creole along in a rough section of Baton Rouge. Tomo knew his way around this part of the country as well as Slocum knew some sections of the West and Mexico. It wouldn't hurt anything to have a second pair of eyes.

Tomo led him down narrow streets leading to the wharfs of Baton Rouge. Better-dressed citizens became scarce. In their place were dock workers and grizzled boatmen, ambling alongside roads leading down to the river, where barges and flatboats and paddlewheelers loaded and unloaded cargo.

Again, Slocum felt out of his element here, away from the West's open spaces. The stench of rotting fish assailed his nostrils, and with so many people living crowded together, the scent of urine and sweat and garbage was so thick in the air he was certain he could cut it with a saw blade.

"I'd hate like hell to live along the river," he said when Tomo led him around a street corner.

"New Orleans be worse," the Creole replied, keeping a hand on the stock of the shotgun he carried under his right arm on a thin piece of latigo strapping.

Tomo watched everyone moving along these streets as though he expected to find someone he knew, or someone he wanted to avoid. His footsteps were slow but certain as he guided Slocum to a section of saloons facing the river,

fronting a street with a crushed-shell roadbed already heavy
with freight wagon traffic.

Slocum smelled smoke, the thicker black swirls of coal-
fed boilers on larger steam boats and woodsmoke from
smaller craft towing barges up and down the Mississippi.

"I wouldn't live here if you gave me the place," he said
as they dodged a mud puddle at a crossroad. "Even if they
gave me this whole damn river I'd give it back to the In-
dians, or whoever wanted to claim it."

"Bad men claim it now," Tomo said quietly, aiming a
thumb in the direction of a drinking parlor bearing a sign
above its doors reading "The Palace." "You go there. Ask
for Ledeaux. Say you want talk business."

"It may take a while. It's early."

"Tomo be outside. You make whistle, Tomo come with
gun fast through back door."

"I hope I won't need your help, but thanks anyway,"
Slocum said, eyeing the front of the Palace. "If my idea's
gonna work, I have to make Ledeaux believe I want to buy
a large amount of raw opium, and I'll have to have a story
to match. If James gets suspicious, we'll be dodging lead
and the girl might be in more trouble than ever. The first
thing I have to do is somehow make an arrangement to
meet with Carl James."

"James be plenty smart," Tomo said, crossing the roadway to reach a boardwalk in front of the Palace. "You
watch close for Joe Wales. He be one who be hard to kill."

"Some's harder to kill than others," Slocum replied as
he made for the Palace's front doors. "I never met one who
could survive a bullet if it went to the right place."

He came to a pair of bat-wings, and after a quick look
over the tops, he shouldered through, stepping away from
the daylight beaming through the door frame behind him.
He saw a room full of bearded, unwashed men seated at

tables, or standing at the bar, drinking from foamy mugs of beer or from shot glasses.

It was because of his better clothing and neat appearance that he drew so many stares, and for a moment all conversation ended in the saloon while its patrons watched him. Then a man at the bar spat loudly into a spittoon and asked, "Who's the fancy dude?"

Someone at a table chuckled. "Maybe this sumbitch is lost," he said.

A gent with tattoos covering both arms looked Slocum up and down from another table. "Is that it, Mr. Fancy Pants? Is you lost?"

Slocum walked slowly toward the bar, his senses keened for trouble. "I'm looking for a man," he said quietly, still loud enough for everyone in the place to hear.

A bartender with pork-chop sideburns and thick eyebrows gave Slocum a questioning look. "An' who might that be, mister?" he asked, making no effort to hide the disdain in his deep voice.

Slocum found an empty spot at the bar and rested a boot heel on a rail beneath it. "A man named Ledeaux," he said, lowering his voice even more. "I've come a long way to talk business with him."

The barman's expression darkened. "Might that be police business, stranger? You've got the look of a law dog all over you."

"I'm no lawman. I want to buy something. Something in particular, and I won't discuss it with anyone else. I need to know the asking price for a certain . . . commodity. I'm from up in Colorado Territory, and this particular commodity is hard to come by in my neck of the woods."

Now the barkeeper's eyes fell to the bulge of a pistol under Slocum's coat. "You're packin' iron. A man who wants to talk business don't need no gun."

"I was told this part of town wasn't safe, and I'll be damned if I'm gonna let anybody take my money belt without a fight." He'd made mention of his money belt for a reason, as bait to draw this Ledeaux into a meeting.

The barman grinned mirthlessly. "You don't look like the kind of feller who knows much about a gun, mister."

Slocum gave him a hard-eyed stare. "Looks can be real deceiving sometimes. I reckon the man who tries to take my poke will find out if my aim's any good." He knew virtually every man in the establishment had been listening to him when he'd made that remark, and he'd said it for a purpose, as a warning.

A gravelly voice from a corner of the saloon spoke. "You're either real tough or real stupid, mister. This ain't no place for a city boy like you."

"Is that a fact?" Slocum asked, turning with his hand near the butt of his .44 to see who'd made the remark.

A swarthy boatman with his elbows propped on a table-top stared back at him. A bottle of rye whiskey rested beside his left hand. His face bore several scars, probaby the result of encounters with knives and fists, and Slocum could tell by the look of him he spelled trouble.

"It's a *fact*," the boatman said, adding emphasis to the last word, a pure and simple challenge.

Slocum pushed away from the bar, sauntering over to the edge of the boatman's table. He stared down into the big man's eyes. "I may look like a city boy to you, sailor boy, but you can add another tattoo to that arm of yours that I go wherever the hell I want, whenever the hell I want, and any son of a bitch who tries to stop me had better be willing to shed some of his own blood to get it done. Tough talk don't scare me. I've heard it all my life, from the Mexican border to the Canadian territories, from the Mississippi plumb to California. Now there've been a few who got lucky, caught me from behind, and fewer still who turned out to be a little tougher than me. But I can count the sons of bitches on the fingers of one hand who made me change directions, and you sure as hell don't look like one of 'em who can get it done.''

Perhaps it was the sound of Slocum's voice, or merely the words he'd chosen, but everyone in the Palace remained silent, watching the two men. Slocum glared down at the boatman and the boatman stared up at Slocum. Neither man moved.

A voice from the back of the saloon said quietly, ''Sit down, stranger. I'll go get Ledeaux.''

Slocum glanced over his shoulder. A smallish fellow in an slouch-brim hat got up from a table.

''Lefty ain't gonna say any more,'' the man assured him. ''He sure don't want no trouble from Ledeaux, an' neither do you. Sit down an' have yourself a drink.''

Slocum turned back to the big boatman called Lefty. Lefty nodded his assent and lowered his eyes.

Slocum found an empty table along one wall, with a chair facing the doors and a corner of the room behind him. He spoke to the bartender. ''Brandy. Imported, if you've got it.''

''We don't sell no brandy down here, mister. It's whiskey, gin, or beer.''

''Bring me a beer.''

The barkeep gave him an icy look. ''We don't got no table service neither. Come get it yourself.''

''Keep it, then,'' Slocum replied evenly. ''I'll just sit here and soak up the atmosphere.''

Now the barman scowled. He took a mug from a rack behind him and filled it with beer from a wooden keg. Slopping foam down the sides, he carried it over to Slocum's table and put it down with unnecessary ceremony.

"That'll be fifteen cents, your highness," he said, giving a mock bow.

Slocum placed a silver dollar on the table. "Keep all the change, for your trouble," he said, fixing the barkeeper with an icy look, meeting the unspoken challenge in his eyes with a challenge of his own.

The barman palmed Slocum's dollar and returned to his other customers. Slocum tasted his lukewarm beer, one of the worst examples of the brewer's art he'd ever sampled, a bitter concoction he scarcely recognized as beer or malt liquor, or even the darkest of ales made in San Francisco.

Most of the Palace's patrons resumed quiet conversations at nearby tables, although a few continued to glance Slocum's way at opportune moments.

Passing time, Slocum lit a cigar, keeping an eye on the door and windows across the front of the place. Whoever this Ledeaux was, he thought, he could inspire both fear and respect from this salty bunch of dock workers and flatboat crewmen. According to Tomo, Ledeaux was the key to getting inside Carl James's plantation, and despite inherent dangers dealing with a wharf-side dice-game hustler who was surely guilty of other crimes, this was necessary to find out what had happened, and what was currently happening, to Josephine Dubois.

He wondered what the girl would look like. According to Bonnie, she was incredibly beautiful, a prize Carl James wanted to keep. James had connections with the Baton Rouge police, enough to keep any official search for Josephine from taking place.

Puffing on his cheroot, Slocum contemplated what it would take to get the girl away from James. Although he'd only had a late-night look at the plantation, he knew it wasn't going to be an easy task. Gunmen like Clay Younger, and whoever this Joe Wales was that Tomo seemed to fear, would make it tough getting her out of there without harm.

A shadow came to the swinging doors. Slocum's right hand moved closer to his hidden gun. A man in a white linen shirt and bowler hat came into the Palace with his trousers stuffed into the tops of his boots.

This new arrival spotted Slocum at once, and Slocum knew this would be Ledeaux. Ledeaux came toward his table, and it was then Slocum spotted a gun tucked into the waistband of his pants.

"Someone say you have business with me," he said, halting behind an empty chair.

"Maybe," Slocum replied. "I'm looking for a man by the name of Ledeaux."

"If I say I am Ledeaux, what business do we have to talk about?"

"My name's Slocum, and I'm down from Colorado Territory to buy something. I was told I could buy it from a man named Carl James, only I had to contact him through you first."

Ledeaux's eyes fell to the swell of Slocum's pistol. "You come to see me with a gun and no money?"

"I've got a gun. And I've got plenty of money to buy what I want. The stuff I'm after costs a fortune up in Denver and the mining camps. I'm looking for the right price, and I brought a gun because I'm a real careful businessman."

"I am also very careful," Ledeaux said. "I bring a gun too, and I see the big Creole standing in the alley with a shotgun who brings you here."

It surprised Slocum that Ledeaux had scouted the building before he came inside, and that Tomo had been so easily spotted. He supposed this was Ledeaux's territory and he would know every nook and cranny of it, every alleyway. "I fully understand using caution in a business deal of the kind I'm seeking," Slocum said. "A man can't be too careful. I don't need any problems with the law, and I don't aim to get shot in the back if I can help it."

"And how do I know you are not the law yourself?" Ledeaux asked.

"You don't. It's a chance you'll have to take, just like the chance I'm taking coming down here. You could simply rob me and toss me in the river. Only that wouldn't be smart for you or this Monsieur James, because I'd planned to do a lot of business with him . . . if the price is right."

"You have the look of a policeman,"

"It keeps most folks away. I dress well. I eat well. And I stay at the best hotels. I'm staying at the Grand Lenier and that's easy enough to check."

Ledeaux drew back the chair. He sat down slowly, still wary of Slocum by the look in his eyes. "You tell me what it is you wish to buy, and how much you want."

"I want raw, uncut opium. I won't know how much I'll buy until I hear a price and see the goods. I won't buy black tar or powdered sugar."

"Perhaps we may have something to discuss," Ledeaux said.

10

"Why do you wish to speak to Monsieur James personally?" Ledeaux asked, leaning over the table, speaking quietly. "I can show you samples of what you want to buy and give you the very best price he can offer."

"I like knowing the folks I'm dealing with," Slocum replied. "It's just good business. I'm a pretty good judge of character. When I look a man in the eye, I know who, and what, he is."

"The opium should be all that matters. The quality of what you are buying."

"Not enough. If things work out, I intend to buy from him on a regular basis. Those mining camps up in Colorado are full of opium dens, mostly run by Chinese. They get big money for a bunch of stuff that's cut mighty thin. I can make a nice profit and provide better stuff, if the opium James has got is good."

"It is the best. Raw. You can see for yourself. But it is

not possible to meet Monsieur James. He is a very busy man.''

''Then he's too busy to need my money. I meet him, and see what I'm buying, or it's no deal. I'll have enough problems getting it to Colorado. I'd buy laudanum, if he's got it. And I'm not talking about a bottle or two. Colorado Territory is wide open right now, crawling with miners who have a pocketful of gold dust and no place to spend it. A whiskey tent and an opium parlor can make a man rich, if he's careful.''

Ledeaux frowned. ''I will have to speak to Monsieur James about this.''

''I expected as much. If he's a careful man, he'll want to know who he's doing business with himself. We can talk. He can check on who I am. It's all very necessary. Otherwise, I'm not interested.''

Ledeaux seemed uncertain. ''I will talk to him tonight. If he agrees, someone will contact you at your hotel. If you do not hear from me, then your proposition is not satisfactory. That will be the end of it.''

''I understand,'' Slocum replied, knowing what he needed to do to cover his tracks. An old friend owned a gambling establishment in Denver, and if Slocum sent him a wire this afternoon, Charlie Jenkins would send a telegram to Carl James saying just about anything Slocum wanted him to say, backing up his story about a few mining camp whiskey tents, perhaps up near Cripple Creek, a part of Colorado Territory Slocum knew well. ''I can give him some names of people who know me. References, you might call them, so he can check on me before we do business. But I want it made clear I won't be a buyer until I see the goods, and talk to the man I'm buying them from.''

''I can only tell Monsieur James what you want,'' Ledeaux said offhandedly. ''If he agrees to talk to you, someone will come for you at the Grand Lenier.''

Slocum nodded. ''Then if we've finished our discussion, I'll be on my way, hoping to find someplace in Baton Rouge where they sell a respectable glass of beer. This is the worst shit I ever tried to drink. It reminds me of dirty bathwater.''

Ledeaux stood up as Slocum left his chair. They eyed each other a moment, sizing each other up. Ledeaux was a wiry man of thirty, Slocum guessed, and by his sure movements he would likely prove to be a dangerous adversary.

''Perhaps your Creole friend out in the alley can direct you to one of the city's finer places,'' Ledeaux suggested. ''My boys could have killed him easily a moment ago, you know.''

Slocum glanced to a side window. ''Don't be too sure of that assumption, Ledeaux. The big Creole might fool you. He killed a man on the way up here. Gutted him with a knife before you could blink and fed him to the alligators, and I hear he's a dead shot with that cannon he carries under his arm.''

''This was one thing puzzling me, Mr. Slocum,'' Ledeaux said. ''Where did you make the acquaintance of a Louisiana Creole if you are from Colorado?''

Slocum was thinking fast to come up with an explanation that would fit. ''He works for a friend of mine, a lady who used to run a whorehouse out in West Texas. I guess you'd call him her bodyguard, a watchdog. I told her I needed someone who could handle himself while I was in strange country I'd never traveled before.''

''This woman. Who is she?''

Slocum couldn't give Ledeaux a truthful answer, or a connection between Bonnie and Josephine Dubois might be revealed. ''If I told you that, you might contact her and offer her more money to have him knife me in the back. I like things just the way they are. You can check on me in Denver, if Monsieur James has the inclination. But there are some things about me you don't have to know, like who the Creole works for. I'm careful around his type. He'd kill me in a heartbeat if the price was right, if the lady he works for gave the order. I know his kind, even though I never met a Creole before. A man who kills for money don't come in just one size or color.''

Ledeaux grinned crookedly. ''You are a wise man, Mr. Slocum. Those very same kinds of men work for me, and for Monsieur James. It is wisdom never to turn your back on one of them, and never to allow them to sell you out for a higher price. A woman who runs a whorehouse cannot be trusted, and neither can the man who has taken her money to protect her.''

''Then you understand why I can't talk about him.''

''I understand. But if Monsieur James allows you to have a business meeting with him, the Creole will not be allowed to be with you.'' .

''Suits me,'' Slocum replied. ''I hadn't planned to let him see how much money I'm carrying anyway. I'll be at my hotel after dark. Tell Monsieur James I'm ready to do business . . . if he has the right kind of merchandise, at the right price.''

''If a meeting can be arranged, someone will contact you,'' Ledeaux promised, wheeling away from Slocum's table. He gave the bartender a nod and crossed the room, walking out without saying a word to anyone.

Slocum waited a moment, feeling the stares of patrons. Then he ambled across the floor and stepped out into a crowded street as gray clouds darkened the skies above the Mississippi.

He saw Tomo standing in dark shadows beside a corner of the building watching him move down the boardwalk.

Slocum wondered idly if Ledeaux had been correct—could some of his henchmen have killed Tomo so easily?

"Let's find something decent to eat," Slocum said as he and Tomo made their way back toward the center of town.

"I show you," Tomo said. "Crawfish gumbo, jambalaya full of shrimp, oyster, crab, an' chicken. Be plenty hot. Taste good. Ol' Cajun woman fix. I know dis place."

"Sounds like a bellyache to me," Slocum said, "but I'm game for damn near anything, so long as I can find a good bottle of brandy to go with it."

Tomo grunted. "Brandy too sweet. Be woman's drink. Tomo like Jamaica rum."

"Did you see Ledeaux come to the Palace?" Slocum asked as they turned toward an older part of town where rows of smaller shacks lined narrow roads.

"Me see. Me see two men also who think I no see them in alley. They think maybeso they kill me. I be ready, only they don't do nothing. Just hide. Watch me like I don't see them."

It was an answer to Slocum's question. Tomo was not quite as easy to ambush as Ledeaux figured.

The place was called Maw-Maws, a run-down clapboard building with a short fishing pier built above the Mississippi. Its patrons were mostly Negro and Creole and persons with skin the color of Claudette's—she had called herself a quadroon. Slocum was the only white man in the place and dressed the way he was, he felt uncomfortable. Delicious smells coming from the kitchen, however, quickly put him at ease, as did the brandy he'd bought along with a handful of cigars at a mercantile they'd passed along the way. Tomo drank from the mouth of a bottle of rum, his shotgun resting against the wall beside him. A dark-skinned girl of twenty or so had taken their order for jambalaya, corn fritters, and fried catfish.

Slocum noticed how everyone seemed to be avoiding them, and he wondered if it was Tomo's presence or his own at Maw-Maws that made patrons wary, ill at ease. Now and then he'd catch a man staring at them surreptitiously, then looking away.

"They aren't too fond of me in here, the locals," he said, toying with his glass of brandy while puffing a cigar.

"White folks no come here much," Tomo explained. "It no be good place for white man after dark."

"I think your shotgun is making some of them nervous."

"Some knows me, what I done 'fore I work for Miss Bonnie."

"And what was that, Tomo?"

"I work dis river. Kill some men. Folks talk."

"It gave you a bad name."

Tomo agreed, nodding his head. "Mos' folks know dis river be bad place. Plenty bad men. I kill some. Now they say I be bad man too."

"Ledeaux said his boys could have killed you in that alley anytime they wanted."

At that, Tomo grinned momentarily. "Be two. I see one look out dis window real careful an' he got pistol. One stay back so he think I no see him. He got big knife, maybeso pistol under his shirt. I think I kill one in window first, then shoot other quick if they come."

It was comforting to know Tomo had seen Ledeaux's men and knew what to do. "I appreciate the skills of a cautious man," Slocum said. "I figure we'll need everything we've got if we try to take that girl away from James."

"Swamp be best way. Take little boat, come through bayou in dark. Kill guards quiet with knife. No shoot gun till we get to big house."

"My way may be easier. And there's no alligators. I'll see what I can find out about her if they let me visit James to talk business and get the lay of things inside the house. If I get the right chance I'll grab her and make for my shotgun and pistol in the fork of that tree. Ledeaux already warned me I'll be disarmed before I meet with his boss. No guns. I'm sure I'll be searched thoroughly. They might miss my derringer if I keep it strapped to my ankle inside my boot, but that's only two shots and no range to speak of."

"No be enough kill Joe Wales," Tomo insisted.

"We'll see. Until I meet this Wales, I'm of the opinion he dies just like anybody else."

Their waitress arrived carrying a tray laden with steaming bowls of a soup-like substance full of rice and other things Slocum did not recognize, smelling strongly of spices and garlic and onion.

He noticed a jar with a spoon in it containing a red sauce with a faintly sweet odor that also burned his nostrils. "What is that?" he asked Tomo as the food was placed in front of them along with a platter of fried corn cakes.

Tomo eyed the jar, then began spooning it into his bowl of jambalaya. "Be blood of red pepper," he said. "Make tongue burn long time."

"Then why are you putting so much of it in your stew?" he asked.

"Taste good. Hot food be good as hot woman."

With lingering doubts, Slocum added a few spoonfuls of red pepper sauce to his bowl. When he tasted it, he understood that Tomo was given to understatement. His nose immediately started to run when the fires of Hell exploded in his mouth. "Damn, but I do believe that's hotter than the *salsa* down in Mexico."

Tomo dipped a corn fritter into his jambalaya. "You get used to it," was all he said.

Reluctantly, Slocum spooned the contents of his bowl into his mouth, discovering that after its initial burning, the red pepper sauce added wonderful flavor.

To keep his tongue from bursting into flame, he drank more brandy from time to time. He was drawn to the jambalaya's distinct flavors even though they set his mouth and lips on fire. "I'll be sick for days," he said contentedly, downing the last of his meal.

Tomo glanced out a side window. "Maybeso we no live that long," he said. "Depend on Monsieur James. An' Joe Wales."

"You're too superstitious," Slocum said, half joking about it.

"I see dead men walk. Voodoo curse make dead rise up from ground. Joe Wales got eyes like snake, voodoo witch say. She say he already be dead."

"Ain't possible, Tomo, despite what you believe. When a man is dead, he's dead, and he don't climb up outta his grave no matter what kind of curse you put on him."

"Voodoo woman put pins in rag doll. Say voodoo words kill him quick. Wales no die. He 'spose be dead man now, only Wales walk like everybody else."

"Why put pins in a doll?"

"Way of Old Ones. Long time ago, voodoo witch say put pins in doll with face like enemy. Say voodoo curse many times. Be pretty quick enemy die."

Slocum wagged his head, cooling his mouth and tongue with a third glass of brandy. "I don't aim to put no pins in Mr. Wales. If he gets in my way getting that girl away from Carl James, I'll see how far he can walk with a few bullet holes in him."

11

Claudette was waiting for him at the top of the stairs when he got back to the hotel at dusk, after he'd wired Charlie Jenkins in Denver asking him to provide a good story, that Slocum was a saloon owner up in Cripple Creek, if anyone from Louisiana inquired. Claudette's hair was combed and she wore ribbons in it, but the look on her face was not happy.

"How come you put fifteen dollars in my handbag last night, Mr. John?" she asked. "I ain't no scarlet woman."

"I wanted you to have money to buy a nice new dress. I never once thought of you as a scarlet woman or anything of the kind. Consider it a present, not a price paid for the time we spent together."

"My mammy say I have to give it back. She kept askin' me where I got so much money, an' I told her this nice man stayin' at the hotel must have put it in my handbag when I wasn't lookin' at what he was doin'."

"I want you to keep it. I want you to buy a dress with it."

Claudette rattled the silver dollars in her fist. "It makes me one of them crib women, on account of what I done with you. I didn't do it for money. This money makes me a whore."

"No, it doesn't. It makes you the owner of a new store-bought dress because I decided to give you one." Slocum saw tears in the corners of her eyes. "It was a present and nothing more than that."

"I can't take it. It'd be wrong."

"I would have bought you the dress myself, only I don't know what size you wear, or anything about women's dresses. I gave you the money so you could choose the one you liked best."

"How come you didn't tell me?"

"I wanted to surprise you. I hoped it would make you feel happy when you found the money. Now I see you're crying, and that wasn't what I wanted at all."

"You made me out to be a whore by givin' it to me."

He reached for her shoulder. "That was never my intention. I wanted you to own something you wanted. If I'd thought of you as a whore, I would have asked your price beforehand."

Claudette lowered her eyes. "My mammy says it makes me a fallen woman, to take money from a stranger."

He felt sorry for her, and tried to console her. "I need a bath. Bring me some hot water and clean towels. You're earning the money I gave you. Try to think of it that way."

"But I got naked in bed with you, an' we made love."

"I hope that happened because it was what you wanted to do, not because you expected any money."

"I never expected no money. When I got home an' found this fifteen dollars in my handbag, I couldn't figure where it came from . . . not right at first. Then I remembered how you asked how much a new dress cost. That's when I figured out where so many silver dollars come from.''

"Fetch me that hot water," he said gently. "Plenty of clean towels, and bring 'em up to the bath. Stop worrying about the money. It's yours to keep, for a new dress. A red one, with a lacy shawl for your shoulders too."

"My mammy won't let me. She'll say I'm a soiled dove."

"Tell her I insisted. That I wanted extra hot water brought up, and I made you take the money." He recalled the possibility of a meeting with Monsieur James tonight, or at least word from a messenger saying James would consider it. "I may have a visitor later on. A business deal I need to discuss."

Claudette cocked her head. "Jus' what kind of business are you in, Mr. John?" she asked.

He smiled. "The business of making pretty women laugh and bad men cry. Now, go fetch me that water."

Her hand moved ever so gently to his stiffening prick under a layer of foamy bubbles. Her naked breasts rested on the edge of the bathtub, puckering where they touched cast iron, nipples erect.

"That feels nice," he said, with his eyes closed.

"You talkin' 'bout the hot water or my hand?" she asked.

"Your hand, the way you curl your fingers around me. It's that your fingers are so soft, I reckon, and they know just where to go."

She stroked his cock several times. "You get bigger when I do this," she said huskily, eyes downcast as though she wanted to see what was going on beneath the bubbles.

"Later tonight, after I have my visitor, why don't you come upstairs?"

She shook her head. "Because of that money. I ain't no kind of whore, Mr. John. You gave me the money an' that changes things."

"How's that?"

"Now, I figure I owe you, an' I don't like feelin' that way with no man."

"You don't owe me anything. You can come up to my room if you feel like it, or go home if you'd rather. But I want you to have the new dress regardless."

Claudette's gaze returned to his face. "My mammy gonna say I shouldn't believe you, that you wanted more than hot water an' a batch of clean towels."

"She's right. I also wanted you. And I wanted you to have that dress."

"So you figure you can buy me, like I'm a whore or somethin' like that?"

"No. I put the money in your purse after we made love last night. You didn't ask for it, and I didn't offer it to you beforehand."

"I wanted you," she said quietly.

"And I wanted you. It was mutual, going both ways. We did what we did because we wanted to. It had nothing whatsoever to do with money."

She smiled. "I liked the way you made me feel, even though it did hurt some."

"I was trying to be gentle. Sometimes, I just can't control myself around a beautiful woman."

"I bet you've got lots of pretty girls waiting for you when you get back home."

"Not all that many. Most women are looking for a man who wants to get married. I'm not of that mind yet. Maybe in a few years I'll want to settle down. Right now, I'm happy being free to go wherever I choose."

Claudette began pumping his prick harder, faster, as a faraway look came into her eyes. "You sure do have a big dick, Mr. John. I swear it made me feel like you was tearin' me plumb in half."

"You wanted it all. You kept saying you didn't want me to hurt you, but when you felt me inside you, it was you who pushed it deeper and deeper."

She closed her eyes, perhaps with embarrassment. "That's because it felt so good."

"Come up to my room later tonight and I'll make it feel good again."

"I can't forget the part about you givin' me the money. It ain't right that I keep it."

"If I'd brought you a new red silk dress, would that have made a difference?"

After a moment's thought, she said, "I s'pose. A dress ain't the same thing as money."

He leaned forward in the tub. "Tell you what. Tomorrow, if I'm not involved with a business meeting, I'll take you to a dress shop and buy you a dress. But I may have a meeting with a man in Baton Rouge named Monsieur Carl James tomorrow."

Claudette's hand stopped suddenly. "Monsieur James? You're gonna have a meetin' with him?"

"I might. Why do you ask? You act like you know who he is."

"He's a terrible man. Everybody in Baton Rouge knows who he is . . . what he does."

"Tell me what you've heard about him," Slocum asked, aware of a change in the girl.

"He kills folks who get close to his plantation, that's one thing for absolute sure. Plenty of folks who got too close to that big ol' house was found dead in the swamp.''

''What do people think he does? You said everybody knows.''

''He sell crazy powder to sinners. Them who smokes a water pipe an' goes crazy after they does it.''

''Opium?'' Slocum asked, to see how much she really knew about James and his operation.

''Some calls it that. Others say it be dust from the devil hisself. Monsieur James keep men with guns around his house all the time, real bad men who kill folks when they get too close to his house. Everybody's afraid of them.''

''I only wanted to know what sort of man he is, this Monsieur James.''

''Terrible man. You don't go there.''

''I may have to go. It's a business deal, but he won't cause any harm to me.''

''You sell the crazy powder too?'' Claudette asked, releasing his prick quickly.

''No. I'm here on another matter.''

She got up and put her hands on her hips, looking down at him with a strange glaze in her eyes. ''I don't believe you, Mr. John. People who go to Monsieur James's plantation are all bad men.''

''I'm not a bad man. I don't deal in opium. I'm here on a private matter, having to do with a girl James took from New Orleans. That's all I can tell you about it. If these gunmen James has working for him are as dangerous as people say, it could be dangerous for you to be around me until I get this out of the way one way or another.''

He looked at her intently. Claudette's demeanor had changed, and she turned suddenly, walking out of the bath.

When he unlocked the door to his room, he sensed something was wrong. Carrying his clothes over his arm, dressed only in his underwear, he reached for the little derringer in his coat pocket and pushed the door open a crack, standing back behind the door frame.

For a moment there was silence. The lamp he'd lit on a tiny table next to his bed shed dim light over the bed, a dresser, and a washstand.

"Who's there?" he asked, peering around the frame with the derringer in his right fist.

He got no answer, yet the feeling lingered that someone was in his room. He glimpsed curtains lifting away from a window on the soft gusts of the night breeze, and he remembered he had not left his window open. Now he was certain he'd had unexpected company while he was taking a bath.

"I've got a gun," he said, thumbing back the hammer on his twin-barrel .32.

More silence.

He waited, and when the waiting lasted too long he pushed the door open wide, aiming for the interior of his room, swinging his derringer back and forth, ready to fire at the first moving target he saw.

Was his night visitor behind the door? he wondered.

"There ain't but two ways out of here, that window or this door," he said. "I'm gonna put a slug in you either way unless you show yourself."

And still, he got no answer to his demand. Taking a deep breath, he steeled himself for whatever, or whoever, was waiting for him inside and lunged through the opening.

He found himself covering an empty room. But as his eyes roamed back and forth, he saw a note affixed to one of his pillows, skewered there by a needle-shaped dagger.

"You bastards," he whispered, closing the door gently behind him, finally lowering his small pistol.

He crossed over to the window, glancing outside. A narrow ledge ran along the row of second-story rooms. When he was sure no one was on the ledge, he peered under the bed, not quite ready to trust his eyes in bad light. Only a chamber pot was there.

He withdrew the dagger and carried the note over to the lamp to read what it had to say.

Mr. Slocum,

Be advised that we must verify your credentials first before you can discuss your proposition. Leave a sealed envelope at the hotel desk with the names of references.

Someone will contact you as soon as your identity can be verified. We do not do business with strangers.

The note was signed in a scrawl, but as Slocum looked at it more closely, it appeared the writer's name was Carl James.

He moved to the window again, looking beyond the curtains at a dark street below. A horse-drawn carriage rattled off into the night a few blocks away.

Slocum went back to the lamp to read the message again, with a growing sense of dread.

"This James is real careful," he muttered, after placing the knife beside the lamp. "But if he thinks he can scare me, he's got a big job on his hands."

He turned down the lamp and lay across the bed. This wasn't his country, the swamps and bayous, and he supposed it was that more than anything else making him uncomfortable. Meeting with Carl James under false pretenses could backfire on him, if they suspected anything. Instead of setting a trap of his own, he might be walking blindly into one. Slocum wondered if it was all worth it, taking this sort of risk for the sake of Bonnie LaRue.

12

He left a sealed envelope at the hotel desk with his name on it, and instructions to the clerk that someone would come asking for it. He'd written down Charlie Jenkins, in care of the Silver Nugget Saloon in Denver, as someone who could verify his status as an entrepreneur, not a lawman—which of course, he wasn't. He'd never been a full-time lawman, even though he'd assisted peace officers from time to time.

Back in his room with a fresh bottle of brandy, he settled in to wait . . . for word from Carl James, and perhaps another visit from Claudette. With the lamp turned down low, he lit a cigar and sipped brandy, remembering the grounds around the plantation, not to mention the alligator-infested swamps around it. Tomo still believed approaching the place by boat was the best way to get in and out, but not being a man with a particular fondness for water in the first place, unless it was found in a bathtub, Slocum was convinced his plan was best.

As he had the night before, Tomo had gone to see a woman to spend the night. The big Creole would not have been welcome at the Grand Lenier. Anyone with Negro blood was turned away from the desk at most better hotels, a byproduct of Southern bitterness over losing the Civil War and having the slaves freed. Old hatreds still ran deep, even after so many years.

Hours later, he turned out the lamp and dozed with his .44 beside him on the mattress, enjoying a cool breeze from the open window where, earlier, a dagger and note had entered his room in the hands of some unknown messenger.

He reminded himself he was in this strange land of alligators and snakes and river people because of Bonnie. Nothing else on earth he could think of could have kept him here for long. He slept without his shirt, to be cooler.

A light tapping on the door prompted his fingers to curl around his pistol grips.

"Who's there?" he asked softly, lifting his Colt off the bed to aim for the door.

"Claudette," a quiet voice replied.

He got up and unlocked the latch, peering out cautiously. "I'm glad you came," he said, pulling the door back.

She slipped into his room. "Some man come to the desk. He take the envelope you leave there."

"I left a message for someone. Thanks for telling me about it being picked up. I'll light the lamp and pour you a glass of brandy."

"I won't stay," she told him. "I won't be your crib girl no more."

"I'm not offering you any money."

"You already done that when you put it in my handbag without me knowin' it."

"I explained before, that was different. I wanted you to

have a new dress. It happens that I've made good money the last few years and money doesn't do anyone any good unless it gets spent on something. You needed a dress and I have extra money. It's as simple as that. I wasn't asking for anything in return, but if you decided on your own to stay and have a glass of brandy with me, it would make me very happy.''

''You got sweet words spillin' outa your mouth, Mr. John, but it don't change nothin'. You gave me money like I was nothin' besides a whore.''

''I never thought of you that way. Why don't you believe me?''

'' 'Cause it ain't so. You figured you bought an' paid for me an' that makes me a whore.''

He tossed his gun on the mattress. ''Have just one glass of brandy with me and listen to what I have to say. Then you can leave whenever you want.''

''You ain't gonna trick me. I won't listen to no more of your fancy words.''

''Just have a brandy. I promise I won't touch you.''

''Just one glass, maybe. But I won't take my clothes off or get in that bed.''

''Agreed. Leave your clothes on. Sit in that chair over by the window and we'll talk a few minutes. I only want you to see that I never intended to pay for you . . . in that way.''

''It's too late to make excuses, Mr. John. I'll have that brandy, an' you can say whatever's on your mind, only it ain't gonna change nothin'.''

He took a glass from the washstand and poured her a generous amount of brandy. She sat on the edge of a straight-backed wooden chair beside the windowsill, staring out at a dark street below as though something else was on her mind.

He poured himself a drink and sat on the mattress. "I know why you're feeling this way," he began. "Perhaps I was wrong to try to show my generosity. But I want you to believe me when I tell you I never meant for the money to make you feel soiled or used in any way. You made me feel good. You are a beautiful woman. I see nothing wrong with buying you a dress because I like you, because I feel something special for you and I want you to have something you couldn't buy on your own. I have plenty of money, and it has nothing to do with me thinking you are some sort of prostitute."

She took a sip of brandy, still gazing out the window. In light coming from gas lamps down on the street below spilling through the opening, she looked so beautiful, he thought.

"I hear what you're sayin'," she told him, "only I don't believe you. Menfolk are bad about lyin' when it comes to talk with womenfolks. That's what my mammy says."

"Your mammy's wrong about me, Claudette. I'm telling you the truth.

"I wish I could believe you. You seemed so nice, an' that big cock of yours sure did feel good, even though it did hurt me some."

"You were on top of me. You made it go deeper because you said you wanted it to feel better."

"It hurt," she replied, looking as if the subject embarrassed her. "Only not too bad . . . not so bad as all that. I wanted it inside me even when it did pain me a little."

Slocum emptied his glass and poured another. "There are all kinds of pain . . . I guess you'd say degrees of it. Sometimes a bit of hurt feels okay if it comes with a hell of a lot of pleasure to keep your mind off it."

"I wouldn't be tellin' the whole truth if I said I didn't like the way it feels," Claudette admitted.

"Then why don't you try again?" he asked. "And this time we won't even discuss money or dresses."

She batted her eyelids. "You promise you won't put no more money in my handbag?"

"You've got my word on it."

Unconsciously, she reached for the top button on her dress and opened it. "It's hot in here, Mr. John."

"We'd both be cooler on a hot night like this if we took off our clothes."

She stood up slowly, placing her glass on the windowsill. "If I do this, you ain't gonna think I'm no kind of whore?" she asked.

"Absolutely not. I'll think you want to make love to me and that really sounds good, because I want to make love to you. You are a beautiful woman. I'd be a fool to say I wasn't attracted to you, and I'd be a liar if I said I didn't want you here in my bed tonight."

Now she smiled. "Them's mighty pretty words. I sure do hope you mean 'em." She unfastened another button, revealing the cleft of her bosom.

He felt his prick begin to stiffen as blood pulsed into his groin. "They're more than pretty words, Claudette," he said as he stood up to open his pants. "I mean them. It's been a long time since I bedded a woman like you."

"You prob'ly say that to all the girls."

"I'm not known for being generous with words."

She giggled and slid her dress off her shoulders, wriggling like a snake shedding its skin until her dress fell around her feet. "You can be mighty generous with that big cock," she said in a whisper, her pretty white teeth gleaming in light coming from the window.

He pushed his pants down to his knees and stepped out of them gingerly, leaving them on the floor. "Come over here,'' he said softly as his blood-engorged cock stood erect, throbbing with the beat of his heart.

She took a tentative step closer, then halted unexpectedly and stared into his eyes. ''Won't be no money in my handbag in the mornin', will there?''

''No money. You've got my word as a gentleman on that, and I'm a man who stands by my word.'' He looked down at her naked breasts, red nipples hardening into knots, and was sure he could smell the scent of her musk.

She came to him then, dropping slowly to her knees, placing her moist lips against the tip of his swollen cock. She made a smacking sound, the kind he would have kissed his grandmother with. Then her tongue flicked out, caressing the head of his member in such a way that he almost lost his balance.

''There's magic in that tongue,'' he said as a wave of desire overwhelmed him.

She took him deeper into her mouth, moaning softly, and at the same time encircling his balls with her velvety palm and her fingers, so gently that at first he wondered if she had them on a satin pillow.

Her tongue probed the length of his shaft, lapping up and down the way a child licks a peppermint candy cane, making sucking sounds while her head bobbed up and down, his cock moving in and out of her mouth with an ever-increasing rhythm.

She stopped suddenly, withdrew his cock, and asked, ''Do you really like it this way?''

''Very much,'' he told her as a slight trembling began in his knees.

She smiled, wetting her lips with her tongue. ''It's so big I can't get it all the way in,'' she said. ''It's too thick down at the bottom.''

''You're doing just fine,'' he assured her, while the muscles in his buttocks tightened. Claudette knew what she was doing with a prick in her mouth.

And then she stopped again, gazing up at him from her knees with a slow smile widening her lips. "You promise not to put it in me so deep this time?" she asked.

"You've got my word as a gentleman, just like I told you before."

Her mouth returned to his cock, feeling warm and wet and wonderful.

Moments later he lifted her by the arms and took her to his bed, placing her on her back across the mattress with his member against the dampened lips of her cunt.

"Not too deep," she whimpered, thrusting her pelvis against the head of his cock hungrily.

He entered her, only a couple of inches, and the warmth of her wet pussy sent his pleasure soaring to new heights as she spread her legs wider.

"Not too deep," she said once more, grinding her cunt over the head of his prick, every muscle in her body trembling with a new level of excitement.

"I gave you my word," he croaked, thrusting as gently as he knew how, despite his passion.

"You did," she hissed, clenching her teeth when the girth of his shaft filled her.

He rocked back and forth, doing his best to keep from going inside her too deeply.

"Give me a little more," she begged now, arching her spine to take more of him.

"But you said you didn't want . . ." Her sighs of pleasure ended what he was saying abruptly.

"Just a little more."

He drove himself into her, another pair of inches, and she was so tight he would have let out a yelp of pain had it not been for her wetness, making his entry easier.

"More," she said, louder.

"I gave you my word."

She answered him by beginning hammering thrusts with her pelvis, enveloping him, stabbing his cock into her moistness with her own efforts.

"I don't want to hurt you," he wheezed, excitement building in his rising testicles.

"Harder!" she cried, and the sound of her voice echoed off the walls of his room.

He obliged her, shoving his prick farther inside the slick walls of her cunt.

"Oh, God!" she exclaimed, hunching faster, harder, with more inner power. "Let me have more! More!"

"You made me promise I wouldn't," he protested, not wanting to break his word to her.

"Forget the promise," she gasped, slamming her groin against the base of his cock.

He gave in, and pinioned her to the mattress with every inch of his prick.

Claudette screamed, and with the window open her voice traveled half a block in either direction down a silent street in front of the hotel.

His testicles erupted and his juices flooded her cunt. He'd broken his word to another woman. . . .

13

He met Tomo for breakfast at a street corner cafe, and told him about the note.

"He came through my window, whoever he was," Slocum said with a mouthful of eggs and ham, "while I was in the bath at the end of the hallway. This ugly frog-sticker knife was buried in my pillow with the message attached."

"It mos' likely be Ledeaux's man," Tomo said. "Thief who work for Ledeaux know how to climb wall like lizard. His name be Louis Fotenot an' he be plenty dangerous. He stick knife in you quick."

Slocum thought about it. "If Ledeaux or James wanted to try to kill me, they've had half a dozen opportunities. I think they only aim to check me out, but they also want me scared so I won't try anything. And I believe their main concern is that I'm with the law someplace, maybe a federal marshal pretending to be a businessman."

Tomo glanced down the street, but only for a moment. "Be a man watchin' us now. He follow us from hotel."

Slocum was amazed at how observant Tomo was, even in a city with crowded streets. "I didn't notice. You've got good instincts."

Tomo was still preoccupied with someone standing in the shadow of a doorway to a dress shop. "Maybeso Ledeaux try to rob you. Man who watch be Louis Fotenot. Ledeaux want to know if you have big money like you say. Ledeaux rob you an' don't tell Monsieur James nothing, keep all for himself."

"But what would Carl James do if he found out? Won't this Ledeaux be afraid of repercussions?"

Tomo grunted, like the answer should be obvious. "Man like Ledeaux only care 'bout one thing. Money. If he think he take your money so nobody know, he do it."

"Do you figure Fotenot came through my window last night to rob me? That doesn't explain the note."

Tomo stirred absently through his eggs. "Thief don't think when it come to money."

"I've got an idea. I'll walk up the next alley and head for one of the banks. If Fotenot is up to no good he'll try to rob me in the alley, and if all he's doing is following me, he'll tell Ledeaux I went to the bank. In order for this to work you have to walk another direction, so Fotenot will believe I'm on my own."

"Miss Bonnie say I stay close, watch out for you."

Slocum tossed his fork in his plate and stood up. "Bonnie knows me, and she knows I can handle myself. After I pay for our breakfast, you walk back toward the hotel. I'm going up that alley alone, and I'll go inside a bank if nothing happens. You wait for me at the Grand Lenier."

"Miss Bonnie gonna be mad if she know 'bout this."

"She ain't gonna know unless you tell her," Slocum replied.

•   •   •

In an alley reeking of garbage and open sewers, he strode through late morning shadows listening closely for footsteps behind him. Huge rats scrambled over piles of refuse overflowing from trash barrels behind some establishments. Now and then he encountered a stray dog searching garbage heaps for scraps, but at this hour the alleyway was deserted. It was still too early for delivery wagons.

Now and then, at cross streets, Slocum glanced over his shoulder. No one was following him, at least no one he could see in the half-dark provided by gray skies thickening overhead.

"He's only keeping an eye on me," Slocum mumbled, crossing over to the next alley with his mind made up to turn for the center of town and enter a bank lobby, just for the sake of appearances, so Ledeaux, and James, would believe he had money in a Baton Rouge bank vault.

It happened so suddenly he scarcely had time to think or react. A dark figure lunged toward him from behind a row of trash barrels. Slocum drew his .44 just a fraction too late for good aim. His finger froze around the trigger as he used the gun for a club, swinging it hard toward the face of his attacker. He heard the sharp crack of bone and teeth when his Colt struck the man's mouth.

"Arrrgh," a voice cried, while in the same instant a knife blade swept across Slocum's right shoulder, missing by inches.

His assailant staggered, and now Slocum could see him well enough to identify him. The man Tomo called Louis Fotenot made a second lunge forward, daggar gleaming, driving it at Slocum's chest.

Aiming for Fotenot's skull, he sent his .44 arcing downward with tremendous force, and when the barrel hit Fotenot's head he heard a thud, feeling the shock of his blow all the way to his elbow.

This time, Fotenot made no sound as he went to his knees, then over on his face and chest in the mud, dropping his knife beside him.

"You damn fool!" Slocum snapped, stepping back, his chest heaving with exertion. "Only a crazy man would come at a man with a gun if all he had was a knife!"

Slocum required a moment to collect himself, until anger got the best of him. He holstered his gun, picked up the knife, and then seized Fotenot by the hair. "Get up, you dumb son of a bitch. I'm gonna show Ledeaux what I'll do to the next stupid fool he sends after me."

It took a moment to revive Fotenot, a slender, willow-limbed man in his early twenties with close-set eyes and a hawk-beak nose. Blood poured from Fotenot's mouth and nostrils, while a gash across his scalp leaked blood into a tangled mane of untrimmed red hair.

Fotenot blinked, tasting blood and mud, running a sleeve over his mouth as he sat in the alley with Slocum staring down at him.

"Get on your feet," Slocum ordered, opening his coat to show Fotenot his pistol. "Walk in front of me to the Palace. I'm gonna show your friend Ledeaux what happens to any son of a bitch who tries to take me down. If you run, I'll kill you and tell the local police you tried to rob me with this knife."

"You may as well shoot me, *monsieur*," Fotenot stammered as he spat out a fragment of one tooth. "This was not Ledeaux's idea. He said you carried money, a great deal of money, and I chose to rob you of it myself. Ledeaux will kill me if he knows I did this."

Slocum's anger was still near a boiling point. "Appears you're a dead man either way. I reckon I can haul you over to city jail and have you arrested for attempted robbery."

"Ledeaux will only kill me when they let me out of a

cell, *monsieur*. I beg you. Let me go. I will leave Louisiana and never come back, if you will only allow me to live.''

"It's more than you deserve, Fotenot."

Fotenot frowned. "How is it you know my name, *monsieur*?"

"The big Creole who was eating breakfast with me recognized you at once. He told me you worked for Ledeaux and that you were probably the one who climbed up to my room last night with the note. Tomo warned me about you."

Surprise changed Fotenot's face. "That was Tomo, the hired assassin from New Orleans?"

"He's from New Orleans, and his name is Tomo. I couldn't tell you anything about the assassin part."

"Everyone in the lower bayou country has heard of Tomo. I wonder why Ledeaux did not tell me."

"Maybe he ain't all that worried about another man's reputation."

"Ledeaux is also a paid assassin. He fears no one, not even the killer Joe Wales." Fotenot wiped his lips again when talking caused more blood to flow.

"I've heard of Wales myself," Slocum remembered aloud. "I'm gonna let you go, Fotenot, just so long as you keep your word and clear out of Baton Rouge. I'm keeping this knife as a souvenir. If I set eyes on you again while I'm here, I'll just shoot you. Won't be any need to explain why."

"No need, *monsieur*," Fotenot replied, scrambling to his feet quickly. He started to back away, not believing, it seemed, that he was being allowed to live.

"Don't worry," Slocum said. "I won't shoot you in the back. That just ain't my way. Now clear out of here, and don't let me find you in this city again or I'll do a hell of a lot more'n bust your teeth and tap your skull."

Fotenot turned, glancing over his shoulder, as he took off in a stumbling run for the end of the alley. He veered at the first cross street and disappeared around the corner of a building.

Avoiding mud and sewage, Slocum made his way to the street and headed for the Palace. As insurance against any chance of a return by Fotenot, he meant to deliver a message to Ledeaux personally.

Walking boldly into the Palace just before noon, Slocum went to the bar, finding the room empty save for the bartender he'd had words with the day before. The barman was busy drying beer mugs when he looked up as Slocum came to the bar.

"I've got a message for Ledeaux," Slocum said, keeping his voice low, even, filled with menace. "Make damn sure he gets it or I'll have to come back." He pulled Fotenot's knife from his waistband and stabbed the tip into the Palace's bar, leaving it quivering there from force of impact, its ivory handle pale in light from oil lamps on the back wall.

The heavy barkeep scowled. "What do you mean by this? That you will stick a knife in his back?"

"I prefer a gun," Slocum replied. "One of Ledeaux's boys tried to rob me just now. I could have killed him, but I let him live after he swore he'd clear out of town. The next son of a bitch who tries to rob me, or stab me, or shoot me, is gonna pay in blood. Tell that to Ledeaux for me."

Slocum turned away from the bar, hesitating when the barman spoke again.

"And who shall I say is the owner of this dagger? I am sure Ledeaux will want to know."

"I was told he went by Fotenot," was all Slocum said as he headed for the bat-wing doors.

Outside, a gentle rain had begun to fall. Slocum turned up his coat collar and tipped the brim of his hat to keep out most of the water as he left the wharfs and saloons fronting the Mississippi. He'd given Ledeaux a clear warning that he wasn't to be trifled with, hoping it would make him seem less like a lawman to Carl James, and more like a buyer interested in opium.

Tomo was waiting for him under the roof of the front porch at the Grand Lenier. Rainfall had grown steadily as Slocum walked across town, and now, as wagon ruts filled with water, freight traffic slowed, yokes of oxen and teams of mules laboring to pull heavy wagons through deepening mud.

Tomo's unspoken question was written on his face as Slocum climbed the porch steps.

"You were right about Fotenot," Slocum said, taking a look behind him to see if he'd been followed. "Fotenot tried to rob me in the alley. The damn fool only had a knife, although it was a wicked-looking blade, about ten inches long, long enough to reach my backbone if he'd gotten the right chance. I swatted him over the head with my gun. Busted a few of his teeth."

"You kill him?"

"I let him live."

Tomo's puzzled expression deepened.

"He swore he'd leave town," Slocum continued. "I took his knife over to the Palace and left it there for Ledeaux, with a message that he'd better not send anybody else to try the same thing or they'd wind up dead."

"Why you let Fotenot live?"

"He wasn't much of robber. He bungled it so badly I almost felt sorry for him."

"Maybeso Ledeaux send somebody else to rob you now."

"I'm not worried. I think he's more afraid of Carl James than he is of me. Fotenot swore he acted on his own, but I wanted Ledeaux to know about it."

"You should have kill him. Nobody in Baton Rouge care. He be bad man, thief."

"I got my message across," Slocum said absently, watching it rain harder. Then he looked over at Tomo. "Fotenot told me something else, something about you. He knew who you were down in New Orleans. He called you a paid assassin, a hired killer."

Tomo's face went flat, expressionless. "Maybeso he make mistake. Dis be somebody else he tell you about."

Slocum grinned. "I don't think so. He sounded like he knew all about your . . . reputation. But that don't matter to me. I don't care what you did before, or what you do after I'm gone. I only want Josephine Dubois away from that plantation in once piece."

"Go by flatboat at night," Tomo insisted again. "Be only way."

A teamster cracked his blacksnake whip over the backs of a team of straining mules pulling a heavy wagon past the Grand Lenier. "I plan to try my way first, Tomo. If that fails, we'll do it your way."

Deep inside, Slocum wondered if it might be his fear of giant alligators keeping him from considering Tomo's idea until he'd tried everything else.

14

With the darkness, the skies cleared. A three-quarter moon hung like a big silver disk above Baton Rouge, the river, and the bayous, bathing everything in pale light as Slocum and Tomo ambled back toward the hotel after eating a meal of tender steak and potatoes at a place called Antone's. A waiter had seemed reluctant to serve Tomo in one of the city's better cafes, until Slocum had informed him that if Tomo was turned away, Slocum would join him. It was the presence of Tomo's shotgun that increased people's apparent fear of him and his menacing looks. Added to that was the prejudice against all men showing Negro blood so common to many places in the South.

When they rounded a street corner, Slocum noticed a canopied carriage parked in front of the Grand Lenier. "Maybe we've got some kind of Louisiana royalty staying at the hotel tonight," he wondered aloud.

Tomo said nothing, watching the carriage closely, slowing his stride somewhat.

111

"Something about that buggy bothering you?" Slocum asked. He had far more trust in the Creole's instincts now.

"Be rich man," Tomo replied. "Maybeso be Monsieur Carl James come to pay you a call."

"He wouldn't send a carriage. . . ." The words died in Slocum's throat when he considered it. "Maybe you oughta hang back, just to be sure. Could be somebody wasn't happy over what I did to Fotenot. Ledeaux may have told James I was a troublemaker. Find a place where you can cover the front of the hotel without being seen. Maybe it's nothing at all."

Tomo ducked into a dark spot between two buildings. Slocum walked to the Grand Lenier's front porch, glancing sideways to see if someone was in the rear seat of the carriage.

Slocum halted his strides when he found a bearded man in a silk top hot watching him from the shadows below the carriage's canopy. He was holding a silver-tipped walking stick. He wore a trimmed beard and a waxed mustache, obviously a gentleman of some wealth by his dress and appearance.

"Good evening, Mr. Slocum," the man said. "My driver is in the hotel inquiring as to your whereabouts."

Slocum turned on one of the steps, facing the carriage. "I don't believe we've met," he said.

"But you asked for a meeting with me. A business meeting."

"Then you must be Carl James."

"I am. Monsieur Ledeaux described you to me." He leaned out from under the canopy to offer Slocum his hand.

Slocum came down the porch steps and took his handshake. "John Slocum. But then, you already know that. I trust you checked my reference in Denver or you wouldn't be here." He examined James more closely, finding him tall, wide-shouldered, with coal-black eyes and thick, bushy eyebrows.

"Mr. Jenkins wired back that you are a profit-seeker of some repute," James replied. "He also said your money was good."

"Shouldn't be much more you care about. I'm not associated with the law in any way, which is what you really wanted to know. I'm not a federal marshal or anything of the kind. In fact, I've had my own difficulties with the law at times. I do understand your caution, however, and I'm gratified. I can't afford any problems getting . . . certain types of merchandise all the way to Colorado Territory. I'm sure you understand what I'm talking about."

James was giving him a hard look of appraisal, eyes roaming up and down Slocum's frame, pausing where the bulge of his Colt .44 lay under his suit coat. "I see you travel armed," James said. "If we are to discuss any business, you won't be carrying a gun."

"That's understandable, just so long as nobody else has one. I've always had this tendency to get nervous when everybody is packing pistols and I'm without one."

James smiled. "Unfortunately, some of my men do carry guns, and they will continue to do so. It's a necessary part of the business I'm in. Unscrupulous men would attempt to take advantage of me, without proper protection. Thus it shall be necessary for you to surrender your pistol before we can begin negotiations for the . . . merchandise you seek."

Slocum wanted to be sure he wasn't walking into a trap. "I think it's fair to tell you've I've deposited most of my money in a bank here. I too must protect myself from unscrupulous men."

"Are you implying I'm a man without scruples?" James asked coldly.

"Not at all. I make it a practice to assume the need for caution until proven otherwise. We've scarcely met. I like to know the man I'm doing business with, and I'm quite sure you feel the same way. We can become further acquainted over a glass of brandy, or sherry. But until I feel certain you have what I'm looking for, at a suitable price, I'll keep my gun and your men can keep theirs."

It was obvious James did not like Slocum's suggestion, but he agreed somewhat reluctantly. "If you wish, we can begin our discussion over a glass of spirits. My driver will take us to a suitable place. I have one requirement. The Creole who escorted you here is not welcome. I'm well aware of his reputation as a paid assassin. An acquaintance of mine says he cannot be trusted in the slightest. I'm also wondering what a businessman is doing in the company of professional killer like Tomo Suvante, and how you came to acquire his . . . services as a guide."

Slocum had to be careful now. An outright lie might be soon discovered. "A friend recommended him to me while I was in New Orleans, although he did say never to turn my back on him. I'm paying him well. Men of his intemperate disposition often can be bought, if the price is high enough. I wanted adequate protection from thieves and highwaymen since I was traveling, with a large amount of currency."

"And where is he now?" James asked.

Again, a lie could prove dangerous. "Just down the street, keeping an eye on things here. He too is a very cautious man, and when he saw this carriage, he suspected something might be wrong. Only this morning a man tried to rob me in an alley on my way to the bank while Tomo was visiting a woman. I was forced to use my gun to discourage the thief on my own."

The door to the hotel opened behind Slocum, and he

turned to see who it was. A man in a flat-brim hat with a gunbelt around his waist came down the steps, giving Slocum a look.

"This is my associate, Mr. Wales," James explained, with a nod in the man's direction. "In many ways he is similar to Tomo Suvante, a professional in the same line of work. It is unfortunate we both need protection of this nature. However, I'm certain you will agree it is sometimes necessary."

Slocum gazed into a pair of pale gray eyes pocketed in a chiseled stone face. This was Joe Wales, the man feared by voodoo witches and even Tomo himself, a fear fueled by the belief that Wales was somehow not quite human. Wales towered above most men at six feet and four or five inches, adding to his fearsome appearance. But it was his eyes that held Slocum's attention, their vacant stare especially, which a superstitious person might believe was proof that the man behind them was dead, or perhaps immortal.

Slocum did not offer to shake Wales's hand, nodding instead.

Wales returned his silent acknowledgment with a nod of his own, spreading his feet apart. Wales was older, in his forties, making him all the more dangerous in Slocum's opinion. A man who survived to the age of forty as a gunfighter had to know his business.

Wales took his eyes off Slocum long enough to speak to James in a husky, clotted voice. "He's carryin' a gun, Boss."

"I can see that. And we've discussed it. Drive us over to the Grayford so that we may become further acquainted. Mr. Slocum may keep his pistol, for now, until he is satisfied as to my honesty." Then James spoke to Slocum. "Please inform your friend Tomo Suvante that he is not to follow us. If you truly wish to do business with me, the

Creole must stay away. I feel it is fair to warn you that Mr. Wales is considered the very best at his job. With only a word from me, he will kill your Creole companion quickly and dispose of his body in the swamp. I trust you will not put this to a test.''

''I'll tell him,'' Slocum replied, giving Wales another look before he turned from the carriage. Wales remained frozen to the spot, his right hand close to a Mason Colt conversion .44/.40 in a cutaway holster. Wales had an arrogant air about him, a stiff spine conveying confidence in his deadly skills. It was the kind of arrogance Slocum despised in gunmen of his ilk, for until they felt the bite of a lead slug pass through them, they radiated a disdain for what they believed were lesser men.

It was all Slocum could do to keep the words inside his mouth as he meandered down the boardwalk in front of the Grand Lenier to tell Tomo not to follow them. The snake's eyes attributed to Joe Wales did not frighten Slocum at all.

He found Tomo in the darkness. ''That's Carl James. I'm going with them to someplace called the Grayford to have a few drinks. James knows about you, and he says not to follow us.''

Tomo was watching the carriage from the corner of a house. ''Other man be Joe Wales,'' he said quietly, but without a trace of fear.

Slocum shook his head. ''I don't care what your voodoo woman says about him. He'll die just as quick as the next man. He ain't nothing but flesh and bone, and if I have to shoot him he's gonna bleed just like anybody else.''

For a moment Tomo did not reply. He continued to watch Joe Wales, until he said, ''Voodoo priestess say he be already dead.''

Slocum felt the weight of his .44 resting against his ribs.

"If that's the case, then I'll kill him again if he goes against me."

The Grayford was an expensive establishment catering to the city's better clientele. Linen tablecloths covered cherrywood tables, and linen napkins were placed in front of every chair. Slocum and Carl James were seated in a dark corner away from the glare of wagon-wheel lamp fixtures hung from the ceiling. Slocum ordered imported brandy. James asked for a glass of cognac.

Joe Wales waited outside with the carriage, leaning against a wall of the Grayford, watching the street. Wales hadn't said a word on the drive across town.

"So tell me, Mr. Slocum. How much of my merchandise do you want to buy? Assuming I actually have this . . . merchandise."

"Depends on the price."

"As you must know, it is sold in ounces. My price is twenty dollars an ounce."

"Too high," Slocum ventured, guessing—he had no idea how much raw opium should cost. "I can buy it for that a hell of a lot closer to home."

"Not in its purest form," James said. "This is juice from the poppy seed itself. Uncut."

"I've heard that one before," Slocum lied, realizing he was on dangerous ground now. If he accidentally exposed his ignorance regarding opium, James would know it immediately. But of greater importance, he had to somehow convince James to let him inside the plantation gates. "I'd have to look at it. Like any other business, there are secrets to the trade and I'm sure you know them. Bear in mind, I'm not accusing you of dishonesty, but in the beginning I must see what I'm paying for."

"I can show you a small sample."

Slocum shook his head. "Not good enough this time. You show me what I'm buying and I'll pay in hard money. It's just good business."

"How much are we talking about, Mr. Slocum?"

He made a show of deliberating. "If it's the right quality I'll buy twenty pounds at fifteen dollars an ounce."

James took a sip of his cognac. "That comes to five thousand dollars. You won't be offended if I ask if you're able to prove you have the money."

"Not at all. I'll show you my money when you show me the goods."

"I prefer things the other way around."

Once more, Slocum shook his head. "I'm the buyer. I come to you in good faith ready to make a purchase. But before I show the color of my money, I must see what I'm paying for. It's that simple, as far as I'm concerned."

"You're a stranger to me, and yet you are asking me to trust you."

"You're also a stranger to me, and you've got this hired gun driving you around, making me nervous."

At that, James grinned crookedly. "You also came to me with a hired killer for a guide. What am I to think?"

Slocum tasted his brandy, trying to appear casual. "You can think I'm being careful, like anyone should be, under circumstances like these."

James leaned across the table, looking Slocum in the eye. "I have this troubling feeling about you, Mr. Slocum, that there is more to you than you are willing to reveal. Nonetheless, I will show you what you want to see. But I must warn you. If at any time I think something is wrong with our . . . arrangement, I will instruct my men to kill you."

"I don't doubt it for a minute," Slocum answered back. "If you are the good businessman I think you are, you'll realize I've got as much at risk as you do. Perhaps more.

I'm out of my home territory. I'm at your mercy, in a manner of speaking. Show me the merchandise and I'll pay you your money, if it is as advertised.''

"Agreed," James said, lightly touching the rim of his glass to Slocum's brandy snifter.

15

He surrendered his gun to Joe Wales, disliking the idea but without options. Wales took his revolver and did not check his boot for the derringer, a bit of luck Slocum hadn't counted on.

The carriage took them through quiet sections of town to the same road he and Tomo had followed on their first night in Baton Rouge, passing bayous on both sides of a crushed-shell roadway. Until now, neither he nor James had spoken after taking seats in the carriage.

"I've heard this place is full of alligators," Slocum said, inclining his head toward a swampy stretch of cypress forest to his right where Spanish moss draped from tree limbs gave things an eerie quality, bathed in silvery moonlight.

"All manner of dangerous serpents," James said. "A cottonmouth snake can reach the size of a man's arm, and its bite is so deadly, men seldom recover from it. Gators are often ten feet long, and when they become man-eaters they fear nothing. Only a gunshot between the eyes will stop them from attacking, even in instances where a human is merely standing close to water. They come ashore at tremendous speed for short distances, and they kill their victims by dragging them underwater until they drown."

Slocum was remembering his recent travels through this same swamp behind Tomo—he didn't want to think about what it would be like to drown in the jaws of an alligator. "I'm sure it does tend to discourage unwanted visitors," he said.

They entered a part of the lane where trees grew close on both sides. Moss, illuminated by moonlight, hung like icicles from branches above them.

"I don't get many visitors," James said. "Not long ago a couple of men showed up uninvited. The official police report says they drowned."

"I take it there might be another cause of death," Slocum observed.

As he had before, James smiled. "These bayous are full of dangers, Mr. Slocum. A man would be well advised to avoid them at all costs."

The rattle of carriage wheels filled a moment of silence, until suddenly Joe Wales drew back on the horses' reins.

"What is it?" James asked, leaning out for a view of the roadway.

"A goddamn gator," Wales replied. "Layin' right up there in the middle of the road. I'll climb down an' shoot the son of a bitch."

"There's no need for that," James replied. "The creature will move in good time."

"I hate the damn things," Wales continued in his rasping voice. "Can't say which is worse, the goddamn mosquitoes or the gators."

"They both serve a purpose," James said, resting against the buggy seat with his hands atop his silver-tipped walking stick. "And they both feed on blood, Mr. Wales. Nature has its own way of providing natural selection. Be patient and the gator will go into the swamp."

Slocum peered at the road ahead. An alligator of eight or nine feet in length lay across the pair of ruts they were following. "It's a big one," he said quietly.

"We have some that are larger," James replied. "Unless they have become man-eaters, they usually give larger animals like a horse, or a man, a wide berth. But one can never tell which ones are man-eaters until it is too late. Thus a reasonable man gives them the benefit of the doubt."

"He won't get any prodding from me," Slocum assured James. Had this same giant alligator followed them into the bayou the previous night? As a means of passing time while the carriage was halted, Slocum spoke to Joe Wales, more than anything else hoping to find out more about a potential adversary. "I take it you're not from these parts, Mr. Wales?" he said, making it a question.

Wales glanced over his shoulder, and in light from the moon his eyes did look unnatural, almost glowing with a light source of their own. "What the hell difference does it make?" he asked in return.

"None, particularly. Just making a little conversation until that thing gets out of the way. You said you hated them and I merely assumed it was because, like me, you're unaccustomed to being around them."

Wales stared directly into Slocum's eyes. "I've been around just about every kind of snake an' lizard there is, includin' the two-legged kind. Don't none of 'em scare me."

James interrupted the beginnings of an unpleasant exchange. "Mr. Wales is from Missouri. He hasn't adapted yet to our wet climate, or our reptiles. But I pay him well and that takes some of the sting out of otherwise unhappy circumstances.''

Wales faced front again, saying no more.

"Can't say as I blame him for not liking it here," Slocum said. "But I suppose anyone could get used to it. The river would be real important to anyone who wanted to move shipments northward. If we can arrive at some sort of arrangement, I'll be looking for a way to send my . . . merchandise as far upriver as I can before putting it on a horse or a mule.''

James looked across the moonlit bayou. "I assure you the Mississippi can be just as dangerous to an inexperienced man who doesn't know what he's about.''

Slocum saw a chance to get a word in to further explain Tomo's presence. "That's the primary reason I need the Creole, to take things upstream so some of my men can pick it up for the ride to Colorado.''

"I seriously doubt that Tomo Suvante can be trusted with a valuable cargo,'' James said. "According to my sources he's a paid assassin, not a riverboat pilot.''

"I was told he's a little of both,'' Slocum answered. "In this part of the world he may be considered dangerous . . . you call him an assassin. Where I come from we've got men who hold very similar reputations.'' Slocum remembered the name of a gunman who had just been sent to territorial prison. "One of them works for me from time to time, a man by the name of Odell Pickett.''

Hearing the name, Wales turned around again. "I've heard of Pickett,'' he said, speaking to James. "He's good, but he ain't all that good.''

James nodded. "Let us hope that Mr. Slocum and I can strike a bargain. Thus there will be no need to find out who is faster with a gun.''

Wales said nothing, watching the alligator again. The big

reptile showed no inclination to leave the road for now.

Slocum decided to add his own implied threat to what Wales had said. "Odell Pickett tells me speed ain't got that much to do with it. Staying calm, aiming real careful, is his way of thinking in a gunfight. A time or two he's been beaten to the draw by a man who was a little quicker, but he doesn't miss and in my book, that's what counts."

One of the carriage horses snorted before Wales could offer a reply, and at the same time the alligator began to crawl across the ruts toward the swamp.

"Patience has proven to be worthwhile," James remarked as he saw the creature move. "I'm a very patient man, Mr. Slocum. I believe in making sure of things before I go too far. I can assure you I intend to be very sure of you before we enter into any business negotiations. And by that I also mean I will make sure you have the money before we do business."

At a pair of wrought-iron gates blocking the roadway, two men carrying rifles came from a tiny shack below a particularly large cypress.

"Open up," one of them said. "It's the boss."

The second rifleman unlocked a heavy padlock and swung both gates wide. In the distance, perhaps a half a mile away, Slocum could see lights from plantation house windows.

James waved to the pair of guards as they drove through, and settled back against the seat. Slocum took note of the men and their guns from the corner of his eye.

"Simple precautions are necessary," James explained. "Men sometimes think they can take what they want by force. I use force, when required, to keep them from it."

"Perfectly understandable," Slocum agreed, examining

a line of trees behind the shack. "A man in your profession, and mine, can't be too careful."

As they drew closer to the house, Slocum could see how truly big it was. Servants' quarters sat behind the mansion, tiny box-like structures . . . vacant now, since the plantation was no longer being used to raise sugar cane, denied the use of slave labor after the war.

"It's a pretty place," Slocum said as though seeing it for the first time.

"It suits my purposes," James said.

As the carriage came nearer to the mansion, several men came out on the front porch. One carried a lantern.

Slocum wanted to emphasize the point that he'd supposedly never been here before. "Are we close to the Mississippi?" he asked, making his question sound casual.

"Close enough," James replied. "If one knows his way about in the bayous, there are shallow streams to follow."

"If I hired a boat and loaded my merchandise here, there is a way to reach the river safely?" Slocum continued, wondering how far the river was from James's boathouse.

James grinned. "There is no such thing as absolute safety in a swamp, Mr. Slocum. If your boatman knows this bayou country, he won't have far to travel to reach the Mississippi."

Slocum's attention was distracted by the shape of a man, no more than an outline in dim lantern light, a man he thought he recognized. He studied the figure a while longer as the carriage drove toward the front of the house. There was something about him. . . .

They came to a circular driveway passing in front of the mansion as Slocum was counting men on the porch. Five men were there, and two at the gate besides Wales, their driver, making the odds extremely high against him.

"Looks like you've got a regular army here," he said

when the carriage made a turn for the front steps.

"All very necessary," James said again. "As you must know, I am in a dangerous business."

"All these men surely cut down on the danger," he remarked, his attention fixed on the outline of the man he thought he recognized.

"Does this worry you?" James asked, giving Slocum a curious look.

"Not so long as they aren't shooting at me," he answered quietly, studying the man in stovepipe boots and flat-brim hat standing back from the others.

"They won't be," James assured him, "just so long as you're who you say you are and your stated purpose for coming here is truthful."

"I'm here to buy raw opium if the price is right, and if the goods are as good as you say they are."

"You won't be disappointed," he heard James say as the carriage came to a halt in front of a wide set of porch steps.

Still puzzled by the familiarity of the man leaning against the door frame of the plantation, Slocum was about to climb down from his seat when he heard a voice coming from the porch.

"Somethin's wrong, Boss."

James hesitated. "What is it?" he asked, gripping the neck of his walking stick.

"I've seen this feller before."

Joe Wales turned around, giving Slocum the eye, and Slocum was sure he'd drawn his pistol.

"Where might you have seen him?" James inquired.

There was a silence. Slocum's heart began to pound as a cold sweat formed around his hat band—he knew that voice, and now he knew who the figure was.

"I saw him down in New Orleans talkin' to Bonnie LaRue a few days ago," Clay Younger said. "He ain't here to buy no opium. He's here to find out about the girl."

16

He heard Wales's pistol being cocked even though he couldn't see it from the back seat.

"Is this true, Mr. Slocum?" James asked. "Are you here under false pretenses?"

"I don't know what girl he's talking about," Slocum replied as sincerely as he could, a note of surprise in his voice. "I did visit Bonnie before I drove up here. She's an old friend from West Texas. She ran a whorehouse there. I spent the night with her my first evening down in New Orleans, but I don't know anything about a girl. What girl?"

James wore a different kind of smile now, a forced expression. "Miss Josephine Dubois, of course," he replied. "Mr. Younger is one of my associates. He was in New Orleans on business, and it would appear he saw you with a close friend of Miss Dubois."

"What has this Miss Dubois got to do with me?" Slocum asked quietly, thinking about the derringer in his boot,

128

certain there were too many other gunmen around him for the little gun to be of any use. "I've never heard of her. Bonnie is great in bed. I see her every chance I get. Tell me how Bonnie and this girl are connected, and why you figure I've got a hand in it."

James stepped down from the carriage seat, looking up at Slocum. "Miss LaRue, as you know, is a madam, a very successful one. She became acquainted with Josephine's family quite by accident. Miss LaRue has large sums of money, and she gives it very generously to a few charities, which is where she met Mr. and Mrs. Dubois, at the Sanitary Commission where nurses are trained. Miss Josephine elected to move away from her family to live with me, and I've been falsely accused of inducing her by dishonest means. As I told you while we were waiting for the alligator to cross the road, two men tried to approach my house recently. It was with the intent of taking Josephine back to New Orleans. I was told the arrangements were made by Bonnie LaRue."

Slocum knew his acting had better be good, for his life was hanging in the balance. "Do I look like a gunman to you?" he began. "Or a man who knows anything about these infernal swamps full of alligators? I'd be the least likely person in the world to make some stupid attempt at rescuing a girl here. I'm here on business and nothing else. You've checked my reference in Denver. I'm not a hired gun, I'm a businessman, and I resent having Mr. Wales point his gun at me now."

"It could all be a clever ploy, Mr. Slocum," James said, "to disguise your real purpose for being here."

Slocum's mouth had gone dry. "What do I stand to gain? I have no stake in any of this affair over Miss Dubois. I have never met her, nor do I know her family. Bonnie and I were lovers many years ago, and it's only natural that I'd see her while I was in New Orleans. I came here to buy merchandise for my drinking parlors, and now I find myself accused of being some sort of bounty hunter looking for a woman I've never met.''

''Perhaps a wolf in lamb's clothing,'' James said evenly, a glance toward Clay Younger. ''Tell me, Mr. Younger, did you see the two of them behave as old lovers should?''

Younger took a moment to reply. ''He kissed her when she came in. They had a drink or two an' left. I was waitin' for Bob, so I didn't pay much attention. But I already told you it was LaRue who hired them two river pirates to come after Miss Josephine.''

James made a closer study of Slocum's face. ''It could be a coincidence, I suppose. However, experience has taught me to be suspicious of apparent coincidences. Climb down, Mr. Slocum, and we'll see if Josephine recognizes you as an associate of Madam LaRue's. If she knows you, or recognizes your name, then I'm afraid we've got a problem here. Unfortunately for you, it may require a permanent solution.''

Slocum came down from the carriage, looking into the eyes of Clay Younger. ''I do remember seeing you standing at the bar in the Delta Queen,'' he said offhandedly. ''It looked like you were waiting for someone. I was waiting there for Bonnie. It was a place she suggested when I wired her that I was coming down to Louisiana on business. We agreed to meet at eight o'clock.''

''You was packin' a pistol,'' Younger said. ''I always notice things like that. Downright unusual for a man dressed up like a city dude.''

''I always travel armed.'' Slocum could hear Wales getting down from the buggy behind him. ''Especially when I'm carrying a sizable amount of money.''

''This is a waste of time,'' James declared. He spoke to

Wales and Younger. "Bring Mr. Slocum inside, and then ask Nellie to go upstairs and bring Josephine down. I want to see if she knows this man."

"Move!" Wales snapped, and Slocum felt the barrel of a gun against his spine.

To appear offended, Slocum turned to James. "If this is the way you treat all prospective customers, then I doubt we'll be in any business deals in the future unless the gun is removed from my back."

"It may only be a temporary inconvenience, Mr. Slocum," James replied. "But I must be sure of you, certain of your motives. Please go inside without further argument. If Miss Dubois does not recognize you as an associate of Bonnie LaRue's, we can continue our discussion over cognac and cigars."

Slocum did his best to seem ruffled by the treatment he was given, straightening the lapels of his coat before he walked up the steps at gunpoint.

Now he had to hope Bonnie had never mentioned his name in front of Josephine Dubois.

She was strikingly beautiful, raven hair flowing over her slender shoulders, her face like a marble statue, a piece of smooth ivory the color of milk. She wore a dressing gown cut low in front, revealing firm, jutting breasts and a tiny waist. She came down a set of circular stairs as gracefully as a ballerina, letting one hand glide down a polished handrail. Her eyes were glued to Slocum's in a curious way, an almost empty stare, as though she were half asleep.

"My darling," James began, bowing slightly. "I want you to meet Mr. John Slocum. Look at him closely, my dear, and tell me if you have ever seen him before."

She reached the bottom of the staircase and hesitated for a moment. "No, Carl. I've never seen him before," she said in a faraway voice, blinking once. A Negro housemaid came down the stairs behind Josephine.

Slocum was stunned by the girl's beauty. He watched her with fascination until James spoke again.

"Have you ever heard his name mentioned by Bonnie LaRue?" James asked.

"No," she whispered. "Not that I recall. I'm very sleepy, Carl. I need more of my medicine, and then I really must go back to bed."

"Of course, my darling. Nellie will see to it that you have another dose of your medication."

Slocum faced James. It was important that he seem indignant now. "I hope you're satisfied?" he asked, arching one eyebrow as he again straightened his lapels.

"Perhaps," James replied. He turned to Wales. "For the time being you can put your pistol away. Mr. Slocum and I will adjourn to my study for a private discussion. Wait outside the door." He spoke to Nellie as Josephine and the Negro housemaid were going up the stairs. "Make a guest room ready for Mr. Slocum, Nellie, and make sure his pillows are fluffed."

"I won't be staying," Slocum said quickly. "We'll talk price and then I'll be heading back to my hotel room."

"Not tonight," James told him, an edge to his voice.

"And why is that?" Slocum inquired.

A flat expression crossed James's face. "I'm still doing a bit of checking on you. Someone who works for me will examine your hotel room tonight, your luggage and personal effects. I must be sure you have no connections to the law someplace. Nothing will be stolen, I assure you."

"I consider that a personal affront," Slocum remarked, his voice reflecting anger. "My word as a gentleman should be enough to satisfy you."

"Ah, yes," James agreed. "But first I must make absolutely sure you are indeed a gentleman. Follow me down this hall to my study. I can offer you the best Cuban cigars, and rum or brandy or cognac from the best bottlers abroad. Don't take offense, Mr. Slocum. This is all absolutely necessary if we are to become joined in a business relationship.''

Slocum gave Josephine a final glance. ''She's a very pretty woman, so I suppose it's easier to understand why you're concerned that someone might try to harm her. I am, however, still disturbed over the treatment I've been shown tonight. If you had doubts, you should have simply refused my proposition and done business elsewhere.''

A door closed at the top of the staircase before James gave him an answer. ''You should expect cautionary measures in any form of illegal enterprise. Let us put it behind us. For the moment at least. Choose your favorite spirits from the bar in my study and enjoy a cigar. We'll talk price. And if nothing is found among your personal effects to cause me undue concern, I will show you the merchandise you seek.''

They entered a huge room decorated with elegant furniture, thick drapes, filigree lamps, a broad mahogany desk, and bookshelves lining three walls. Leather-bound chairs were arranged around an oval table where decanters of liquor glistened in soft lamplight, surrounded by crystal goblets.

''You live well,'' Slocum said upon entering the study, all the while wondering if there might be something in his luggage to give him away, although for the present he couldn't imagine what it could be . . . an old letter, perhaps, or a wanted poster from some manhunt he'd undertaken in the past.

''I'm quite comfortable,'' James said, selecting a chair

across the table from Slocum as Joe Wales closed the door, taking up a position outside in the hall.

Slocum chose a seat, clipped a cigar, lit it with a lucifer, and poured himself a brandy. He wondered if Tomo could be near the Grand Lenier keeping an eye on his room from a distance, or even worse, from the front porch or the back alley. Slocum told himself it was pointless to worry about the outcome now—he was powerless to do anything to prevent whatever happened.

He blew smoke toward the ceiling. "You said we'd talk price and then I'd see what I'm buying."

"Would you care to smoke some?" James asked. "I have quite a selection of pipes if you'd like a sample of what I'm offering for sale."

"I never touch the stuff. It's for folks who don't have good sense, in my opinion. I sell it and make a handsome profit, and the same goes for whiskey and beer. I drink good brandy or cognac—in moderation, of course."

"A wise choice, not to smoke the fruit of a poppy seed. I do not touch it either. It is, as you say, for fools and loafers who have nothing else to do with their money."

Slocum nodded, finally experiencing a sense of relief after the encounter with Clay Younger outside. But now that he had seen James's safety precautions up close, the chances of him getting Josephine out of there without harm seemed more remote than ever. Too many men with guns protected the plantation, and some, like Wales and Younger, would be hard to outwit or outshoot. And Carl James was nobody's fool, Slocum judged. With a gun in his hands he could be dangerous.

Slocum examined the room, paying particular attention to its windows in the event an escape from the study might be necessary in a running gunfight.

"I see you have iron bars over the windows," Slocum

said. "You've turned this mansion into a fortress."

"Only in case fortifications are needed," James replied as he stoked his own cigar. "I've found that money can be every bit as useful as a gun in deterring violence."

"Yet you've hired violent men," Slocum observed. "You see a need for both, obviously."

"Nothing wrong with caution, Mr. Slocum. I have found it to be most useful at times."

"Why is someone searching my room?" he asked. "If I was a lawman working in secret, I sure as hell wouldn't carry a badge in my valise."

"Ledeaux may find other documents to tell us who you really are."

"Then you don't really think I'm an opium buyer from Denver as I've stated?"

"Perhaps. We shall see."

They'd been talking for two hours or more when heavy footsteps sounded in the hallway. James seemed more relaxed until someone knocked.

"Come in," James said, leaning forward in his chair with a frown on his face.

Slocum wondered if it might be Ledeaux, come to warn James about something he'd found in Slocum's room. Again, despite two glasses of brandy, his heart began to beat faster.

A man in rumpled trousers and an ill-fitting cotton shirt burst into the study. He glanced at Slocum first, then spoke to James.

"Somebody blew Ledeaux's head clean off behind the hotel," he gasped, sounding as if he'd run the entire way to the plantation without stopping. "Just left the stump of his neck. It was a shotgun done it, *monsieur*."

James stared at Slocum briefly. "It would appear that Tomo Suvante was watching your room."

"Another thing, *monsieur*," the man stammered, his face now deeply colored by exertion, beaded with sweat. "Whoever done it cut Ledeuax up real strange. Never seen nothin' like it before."

"How's that?" James inquired, remaining calm despite the other man's obvious agitation.

"Like I said, his head was blown plumb off. An' we found his head with half his face blown away, only his dick was stuffed in his mouth. Some son of a bitch cut it off an' put it between his teeth, what was left of 'em. Bloodiest mess I ever did see, an' you know how tough Ledeaux was."

"He wasn't careful enough," James said, with a sideways look in Slocum's direction.

Slocum leaned back in his chair and stubbed out his cigar. Tomo had demonstrated some of the cleverness and skill Bonnie attributed to him. Now Slocum's life would depend on being able to distance himself from the Creole in James's eyes. "It sounds like a pagan practice," Slocum said. "Thoroughly disgusting, to cut a man's genitals off like that. I wasn't warned beforehand Tomo was a heathen . . . if he's the one who actually did this."

"I wonder if you're telling the truth," James said, giving Slocum a hooded stare. "Our negotiations have come to an end until I can find out more."

17

"I'd like to be driven back to my hotel," Slocum said. "You can't hold me accountable for the actions of that Creole. I took him on as a bodyguard of sorts. If your man Ledeaux tangled with him, I'm not responsible."

James shook his head from side to side while Joe Wales looked on, leaning against the door frame with his palm resting on the butt of his holstered gun. The messenger was still out of breath, awaiting further instructions from James while holding a battered seaman's cap in his hands.

"You'll be my guest tonight while I look into things further regarding Tomo Suvante," James said. "I have this feeling now that something is amiss." He looked up at Wales. "Ride to Baton Rouge and see what you can find out. Take Carson with you."

"I don't need no help," Wales replied.

"Take him with you," James insisted, tipping his glass to his lips. "Inform my friends at the Palace of what has happened to Ledeaux, and tell them I've put a price on

Tomo Suvante's head of five hundred dollars.''

Slocum wondered how Tomo would fare now, with half the wharf rats in Baton Rouge on the lookout for him and the five-hundred-dollar reward. ''Is this really necessary?'' Slocum asked after downing his brandy. ''Tomo was probably only doing what I was paying him to do, keeping an eye on my room.''

''I'm afraid it is entirely necessary, Mr. Slocum. I can't have a renegade assassin like Suvante killing off my men. It is a poor reflection on my . . . associates, and my reputation.''

Slocum put down his glass. ''If I'd known I might become a prisoner here, I wouldn't have come. This is a most unprofessional way of doing business.''

''You presented me with unexpected complications. Most men of good character find no need for violence.''

''And what do you call Wales and Younger?'' Slocum asked, in an attempt to turn the tables.

''Simply precautionary, I assure you. A form of protection. They were not hired to perform random killings, only to guard my merchandise.''

Wales took a step into the room. ''I'll kill the Creole an' bring you his fuckin' head, Boss. I'll cut his dick off just like he done to Ledeaux. I could use the extra five hundred.''

James nodded his assent. ''Take Carson,'' he added. ''Ask Mr. Younger to come in. He'll escort Mr. Slocum to his room upstairs and stand watch at the door.''

''You're treating me like a criminal when I've done nothing wrong,'' Slocum objected, making it sound like a serious affront when he was actually glad to have a chance to see the rest of the house. But at the same time he wondered about Tomo. Would Tomo be able to outwit Joe

Wales and another hired gun, in addition to the men from the Palace who would be looking for him?

"As far as I know, you've done nothing wrong," James replied as he got out of his chair. "In the morning, if all goes well, we shall continue our business deal and you can go to the bank to get the purchase price. With an escort, of course, just to be certain there won't be a double cross."

Slocum got up as Wales left the room. The messenger went out behind Wales, leaving the two of them alone for the moment. "I'm quite frankly offended by this discourteous treatment, Mr. James. However, to satisfy you, I'll comply without any further objection. But if we aim do business in the future, it won't be like this. I'll find another source for what I'm looking for."

Before any more was said, Clay Younger appeared in the doorway.

"Take this gentleman upstairs to the north guest room and remain outside," James said to Younger. "I'll have Nellie bring you a bottle of whiskey."

Younger eyed Slocum a moment. "He ain't armed, is he?"

"Mr. Wales took his pistol," James answered. "Show him up and have Nellie bring him anything he desires . . . with the exception of a gun, of course."

"Follow me," Younger said to Slocum, backing out into the hall. The tone of his voice was cold, filled with warning.

"Good night, Mr. Slocum," James said. "I hope you sleep well."

Slocum refrained from making any further comment, following Younger out of the study, taking in every detail of the lower floor of the house without being too obvious about it as they went to the stairway.

At the top of the stairs a long hallway ran the length of

the house with doors opening into the hall on both sides. He followed Younger to a door.

Younger turned unexpectedly, facing him. "You ain't here to buy no opium," he said. "You think you've got James fooled, but you ain't. I know a shootist when I see one. You could say that in my line of work, you need to know who's dangerous an' who ain't. When you came in the Delta Queen that night I had you spotted for a gunslinger."

"You're wrong," Slocum said evenly. "I was simply visiting on old friend who happens to be a pretty lady. I came to Louisiana looking for a better price on the opium those miners up in Colorado want. I'm not a gunman."

"I say you're a liar." Younger said it like he was looking for a fight.

"Under ordinary circumstances I would take offense at your remark."

"You was watchin' me in the mirror the whole time I was at the bar."

"That's because you were watching me and I was worried about being robbed."

"That's a lie an' you know it. You carried a pistol in a cross-pull rig. Like ol' Doc Holliday."

"It's preference rather than having any particular skill with a revolver. It's easier to reach that way."

"You're feedin' me bullshit, Slocum."

Slocum's temper went on the rise, although he checked it as best he could. "I am not a shootist, as you called it. I'm a businessman from Colorado."

Younger opened the door. "Stay put, Slocum, until the boss says it's okay to leave this room. You try anythin' funny an' I swear I'll kill you."

Slocum eyed Younger carefully. "I'm sure you're quite capable of it. But I'll assure you I won't give you any reason to use a gun on me. And as you can see, I'm un-armed, and only a fool would make an empty-handed attempt against a man who carries a gun.''

Younger's eyelids lowered. ''You ain't got me fooled one bit, Slocum. You're a hired shooter somebody sent after the girl at the end of the hall yonder.''

Without realizing it, Younger had just given Slocum some very valuable information, the location of Josephine's room on the second floor.

''I already told Mr. James I know nothing about this girl or why anyone would be after her. You're badly mistaken.''

''I don't think so. Time'll tell.''

For one brief moment Younger's back was turned, giving Slocum a chance to grab his .44. With Joe Wales out of the house, it would be perhaps the best of times to make a play for Miss Dubois and make a getaway.

It was Slocum's anger that made him do it, anger at being called a liar just now. Lightning-fast, he reached for Younger's pistol and snatched it from its holster, giving it a road agent's spin so it was aimed at his adversary.

Younger wheeled when he felt the gun leave his side. But he quickly found himself staring into the muzzle of his own revolver as Slocum drew back the hammer.

Younger froze.

''I could kill you easily now,'' Slocum hissed, rage tightening his grip of the Colt's handle. He placed the barrel gently underneath Younger's jaw. ''All I've got to do is squeeze this trigger and your brains will be decorating Mr. James's upstairs ceiling.'' Slocum grabbed the front of Younger's shirt. ''I'm mighty sensitive about being called a liar.''

Younger stared down at the gun. Then his eyes went to Slocum's face. ''You ain't got the nerve. One shot an' every shooter James has got will come runnin' up them stairs with guns blazin'. You'll be deader'n pigshit.''

Slocum inclined his head. "No doubt about it, with the odds so long. But one thing you can count on, Younger. You'll be the first to find out what a grave is like, 'cause at this distance I can't miss.''

"You're bluffin','' Younger growled, tensing.

Slocum leaned closer to the Missourian's face. "One way to find out for sure, and that's to make a stupid move. I've got nothing to lose. There's a chance I can shoot my way out of here and get through that swamp. But you've got no chance whatsoever of outliving a forty-four slug coming right through the top of your skull.''

"You talk tough,'' Younger said. "I wonder if you're as tough as you sound.''

"Just scratch an itch, or wiggle. That's how you'll know for sure.''

A cloud of doubt began to form in Younger's eyes. "If you pull that trigger, all hell's gonna break loose.''

"You won't be here to see it,'' Slocum promised, nudging the gunman's neck with the gun muzzle. "The only sound you'll hear is the click, when the hammer falls. After that, it's gonna be real quiet, wherever the hell you're going.''

"I knew you was trouble the minute I set eyes on you in New Orleans.''

"You don't know what trouble is unless you don't do exactly as I say,'' Slocum said.

"Even if you kill me, you've got Joe Wales to contend with. He's a stone-cold killer.'' Younger said it with less conviction than before, squirming a little in Slocum's grasp with the gun at his throat.

"You may find this hard to believe, but he don't scare me in the least. I'm accustomed to dealing with bad men, and experience has taught me one thing—that no matter how tough some hombre thinks he is, he dies just the same as everybody else if the bullet is rightly placed.''

"I knew I was right," Younger said, quieter, less defiant now. "I knew you were trouble from the beginnin'."

"Your troubles have only begun unless you show me to the girl's room and do it quietly. It's the only chance you've got of coming out of this alive."

"You're only gonna kill me anyways," Younger insisted. "I got no chance at livin' through this."

"I'm a man of my word, Younger, and I'm giving you my word that if you cooperate, I'll let you live. All I want is to get Josephine Dubois back to her father and mother. If you don't get in my way while I'm at it, you'll live to see another sunrise."

"If you're some hired gun, your word ain't worth a shit," Younger said.

"Perhaps that's your experience. And yes, my gun has been for hire a few times. The way I see it, you've got two choices. Do what I tell you to do, or get fitted for a pine box tomorrow morning."

Younger glanced down the hallway. "She's down yonder, at the far end."

"Start walking that way. This forty-four will be at the back of your head. One misstep, one mistake, and you'll hear this little clicking noise, and maybe a cracking sound when the slug passes through your brain."

"You'll never get out of here alive," Younger warned as he made a slow turn for the end of the hallway.

"I've been told that before," Slocum answered, moving the gun muzzle to the base of Younger's head. "Somehow, the gents who said it wound up being wrong. Now move!''

18

Tomo stood quietly, watching two riders pass through gates leading to the mansion. He recognized one of them. Although he did not actually fear Joe Wales, he was disquieted when he saw the gunman with snake's eyes leave the plantation. Voodoo magic was not superstition, as John Slocum believed it was. Tomo had seen dead men walk during a voodoo ceremony when he was a child, and when the bodies arose from their graves, parting the earth to lift the lids from their coffins, everyone who saw it knew it could not have been trickery. A voodoo priestess had said that dead men truly walked among the living, and anyone who'd had doubts found them quickly dispelled when they saw corpses rise from the ground that night. And when the voodoo witch first set eyes on Joe Wales, she'd warned that magic would do nothing to stop him, for he was already dead, possessed by evil spirits with the eyes of a serpent.

Standing near the road, Tomo listened to the two men talking.

"We ain't gonna tell nobody else 'bout the five hundred bucks to kill that Creole," Wales said, saying it quietly as they passed near the tree where Tomo was hiding. "We'll kill the sumbitch ourselves an' split the reward."

"Suits the hell outta me," the other horseman said, kicking his roan gelding to a trot. "Did I hear Pierre tell you the Creole shot off Ledeaux's head?"

"An' whacked his dick off so's he could stuff it in his mouth," Wales replied. "That's what Pierre tol' the boss just now."

Their voices were fading away as the second gunman said, "When we find that half-nigra bastard we'll do the same to him."

Tomo slipped away from the cypress grinning savagely. He had truly enjoyed killing Ledeaux. Ledeaux was the type of Cajun found on all southern Mississippi wharfs, a tough-talking knife-wielding bully who believed he was invincible. When a full charge of shotgun pellets tore through his throat, he'd been coming for Tomo with a pistol. Had Ledeaux only carried a knife, it would have been good sport to cut him up with the Bowie, make him bleed and suffer the way he had done to so many of his victims, according to loose talk among dock workers along the river.

Ledeaux's head had gone flying off his neck as though it were severed by an executioner's axe, rolling down the alley behind the Grand Lenier like a misshapen ball, wobbling, leaving a trail of dark blood until it came to a halt in a sewer ditch, a proper place for the head of a man like Ledeaux. Cutting off his pecker and stuffing it into his mouth had been an afterthought, an old Indian ritual someone had told Tomo about long ago. It had seemed fitting somehow.

Tomo swung aboard his chestnut and reined in behind Wales and his partner, keeping a safe distance in the dark.

He had just learned that Monsieur James was offering five hundred dollars for his death, as revenge for what had happened to Ledeaux. James was indeed a generous man with his blood money.

Tomo worried some about Slocum being alone at the plantation for a few hours while he followed the two gunmen into Baton Rouge now. In many ways Slocum appeared to be incapable of taking care of himself, seemingly knowing nothing about survival away from a city. Yet there was some indefinable thing about him, the way he carried himself perhaps, that made Tomo wonder. Was he as brave as he sounded? Or simply brash, the way Ledeaux had been until his head was blown into a sewer.

Following the two men without being discovered was easy, for they paid too little attention to their surroundings. But in the back of his mind Tomo wondered if Wales knew he was being followed. A creature from the grave would not worry about someone made of flesh and blood making an attempt on his life.

Tomo deliberated his chances as they came closer to lights from the city. If he tried to shoot Joe Wales and his bullets did no harm, then what was he to do? The witch had said it was not possible to be protected from the dead who walk. They sought out their prey and killed them. Guns and knives were of no use, and neither were magic spells or garlic cloves, or any arrangement of chicken bones inside the Magic Circle. Men of flesh and blood were defenseless against the dead who walk. Tonight, Tomo would find out if Wales was truly arisen from a grave—he must take the chance, after giving his word to Miss Bonnie.

Wales and his companion rode into the outskirts of Baton Rouge, and now Tomo knew he had to be much more careful. They were looking for him and he was behind them. Somewhere, the tables would turn.

It was time to leave his horse with Lizbeth, the girl he'd seen while he and Slocum were here. Stabling his chestnut in a barn behind her tiny shack, he would then be on foot, harder to see, making it easier for him to use the darkness to hide.

In deep shadows blanketing the alley behind the Grand Lenier Hotel, Tomo watched Wales dismount. They had ridden back and forth twice looking for Tomo, covering every inch of the alley with pistols drawn, as though they expected to find him there watching Slocum's room.

"Hold my horse," Wales said. "I'll go round to the front an' see if he's inside, maybe upstairs where he thinks he can keep an eye on things better." He holstered his gun and swung down.

"I'll come runnin' if I hear any shootin'," the man named Carson promised.

Wales looked up at his companion. "I won't need no help," he said, saying it so softly Tomo barely heard him.

Wales walked into a narrow opening between the hotel and a building with darkened windows, his boots making a soft sound in the mud below the Grand Lenier's eaves.

Tomo waited, crouched behind a section of rusting wrought-iron fence near the end of the alley. When he'd given Wales enough to time enter the hotel, he crept forward on the balls of his feet, quietly cocking both hammers on his old Parker twelve-gauge, a gift from his father when he was a small boy, one of his most treasured possessions. He'd lost count of the number of men he'd killed with it years ago, and seldom thought about the lives he'd taken. Killing was necessary for a boatman in those times, as necessary as his next breath of air. Only after he'd gone to work for Miss Bonnie had he been able to live a more peaceful existence, manhandling a few rowdy drunks, making sure no one threatened her life or her valuables, an easy task compared to things he'd done before.

Carson seemed intent upon the hotel, expecting gunfire when Wales got inside. Thus he never heard Tomo's careful approach to a spot in the alley behind him. To keep his promise to Bonnie, he would have to kill Carson and do it quickly while Joe Wales was inside, reducing by one the number of men who stood in Slocum's way getting the girl back to New Orleans.

"*Bon soir*," he whispered, wishing the gunman a good evening in French before he blasted him into eternity.

Carson wheeled, clawing for his pistol. Tomo brushed his finger against one of the Parker's triggers.

The clap of exploding gunpowder resounded off the hotel's rear wall, spooking both horses as a bright muzzle flash briefly illuminated the alleyway. Carson was torn from his saddle as his horse lunged to the right, and above the shotgun's roar Tomo heard a scream.

Carson was flung against the masonry and brick of the Grand Lenier, pinioned there momentarily by the force of speeding lead, blood splattering around him. One horse galloped east trailing its reins, while the other bolted west, racing past Tomo, snorting with fear. Before the echo of the gunshot died, Carson slid down the wall leaving a bloody smear in his wake, crumpling in a heap beside a trash barrel.

At the same time Tomo was running—he didn't need a closer look to know Carson was dead, torn almost in half by buckshot at very close range, his spine doubtlessly shattered. All that mattered was there was one less hired gun to battle over Miss Josephine Dubois now, even though the worst of them, Joe Wales, was still alive.

Tomo darted into the shadows of an empty side street as he removed the spent shell from one chamber, loading another, all the while running as hard as he could toward Lizbeth's shack to saddle his horse. Wales would be searching for him, and if he truly had the supernatural powers afforded the dead who walked, he would find Tomo no matter where he hid. But Tomo would ride back to the plantation, and if Wales was merely a mortal, Tomo would be in the most unlikely spot possible. Wales would never look for him there. It was a gamble either way.

As he ran through a quiet residential part of town, it was almost as if he could feel Wales behind him. Was he allowing his imagination to play tricks on him? Or was a dead man stalking him across Baton Rouge, a man who could not be stopped by any weapon known to mortals?

Racing into a poorer section of the city, he followed dark alleys to Lizbeth's cabin and ran up to the back door, tapping lightly.

"Who is it?" a wary voice asked.

"It be me. Hurry an' let me in."

A pretty quadroon woman in a faded yellow dress opened the door for him. Her brow immediately furrowed with worry.

"What's wrong, Tomo?" she asked as he hurried inside to get his saddle and bridle.

"The Dead One comes. He come to kill me. I shoot dis man who ride with him."

"The Dead One?" Lizbeth wondered. "Who dat be?"

"Joe Wales. Queen Adriana say he got eyes of a snake an' he come from a grave. She warn me stay away from him."

Lizbeth's eyes widened. "He come here?"

"Maybeso he know I be here. I saddle my hoss an' ride off quick so he don't do nothin' bad to you."

"Oh, Tomo! Why you get crossways with dis kind of folks?"

He hoisted his saddle and blanket with his bridle draped on his forearm. "I do it for dis nice lady who give me job in New Orleans. Now you turn out lamp, an' don't open dis door for nobody tonight. Act like ain't nobody here."

She stood on her tiptoes and kissed him as he was about to leave.

"Put out that lamp, woman!" he snapped, peering out into the night before he went down Lizbeth's back steps with his shotgun resting against his hip, the saddle over his shoulder.

He felt tiny hairs bristling on his neck as he was saddling the chestnut, and now he was certain Wales was close. An inner voice told him he'd challenged the mightiest of evil powers this night. Slocum was a fool to call voodoo superstition, and if he went up against Joe Wales he would find out, too late, that there was more to black magic than he realized.

Tomo rode quietly away from the little shed behind Lizbeth's shack, his shotgun ready. Every shadow, every dark corner could be a hiding place where instant death awaited him.

Two blocks from the shack, he risked urging his horse to a trot, feeling an evil presence more strongly than ever. A dog began to bark when it heard his horse's hooves, and he knew this sound would draw Wales to him the way vultures are drawn to a kill by scent.

"He ain't but jus' a man," Tomo whispered to himself as his horse carried him between rows of dark houses.

The infernal dog kept barking, angering Tomo enough that he gave thought to finding it and killing it.

Glancing over his shoulder almost continually, he rode for the swamps with a sweat covering him from head to toe, not the sweat of labor, but rather the sweat of fear.

"I ain't scared of nobody on dis earth," he said aloud at the outskirts of the city, but even as the words left his lips, he knew it was a lie. He was afraid of Joe Wales, and no amount of talking to himself would change things.

19

Slocum kept Younger's pistol against the base of his skull as they moved quietly down the lamplit hall. Slocum knew any number of things could go wrong. The Negro housemaid might see them and sound the alarm, or one of James's gunmen could spot Younger with a gun to his head being paraded across the top floor of the mansion. Within seconds, shooting would start and there was no way down except the spiral staircase. Even then, Slocum and the girl would have to get past two guards at the gate, unless they navigated the swamp on their own . . . an unlikely prospect with the woman in tow and Slocum's healthy respect for alligators.

"Open the door," he whispered in Younger's ear as they came to a door at the far end of the hallway. "And be real quiet or this gun goes off."

"You'll never make it out of here alive," Younger said, his lips curled in a snarl.

"Maybe not, but you can count on one thing . . . you'll be the first to die."

"That bitch in New Orleans must be payin' you a hell of a lot of money for this."

"We haven't discussed money," Slocum answered as Younger reached for the doorknob. "She's just so damn good in bed that price was never talked about."

"You gotta be crazy."

"I am. Crazy about Bonnie LaRue, and just crazy enough to blow a tunnel through your head unless you do exactly what I tell you to do."

Younger twisted the knob. "There ain't no place west of the Mississippi you can hide from Carl James if you take his woman. He'll hunt you down like a chicken-killin' dog with the best guns money can buy."

"I'm willing to take that chance," Slocum said as the door swung inward. "Like I said, Bonnie has got real good loving and it's worth the risk."

The bedroom was lit by a small coal-oil lantern. Underneath a canopy above a four-poster bed, Josephine Dubois lay sleeping soundly. Open windows on either side of her bed had lacy white curtains fluttering gently in a night breeze.

Slocum pushed Younger through the door and closed it behind him. Without a sure way to restrain Clay Younger and keep him out of a fight that was almost certain to come, Slocum had but one choice.

As quickly as he could he swung the barrel of the gun and struck the back of Younger's head, sending the gunman crumpling to the floor with a groan.

Slocum glanced up to see if the noise had awakened Josephine, and he found her eyelids closed.

"She's gonna make some noise," he whispered, leaving

Younger where he fell to cross over to the bed. When he awakened her, she was likely to scream.

In a corner of the room a wardrobe cabinet stood open, and hanging on several pegs was an assortment of brightly colored silk scarves. He would have to tie one over her mouth until he got her downstairs and away from the house, and use another to tie her wrists behind her.

He took two and came over to the bed, still holding the .44 belonging to Younger. "Wake up, Miss Dubois," he said in a low voice, touching her shoulder.

He got no response, and tried again. "Wake up, Josephine. I have to take you with me."

The girl's eyes fluttered open. For a moment she stared at the ceiling, before her gaze turned to Slocum.

"Who are you?" she asked sleepily. "Haven't I seen you somewhere before?"

Slocum wanted to reassure her if he could. "Yes, it was earlier this evening, downstairs. Monsieur James asked you if you'd ever seen me before."

Just then, Josephine noticed the gun. "What are you doing?" she asked, raising her head slightly.

"I'm taking you back to New Orleans. Your mother and father want you away from here."

She opened her mouth to scream, and he covered it with the palm of his hand. "Don't yell, Miss Dubois. A lot of people are liable to get killed unless you cooperate with me."

Her head fell back against a goose-down pillow, and for the moment Slocum removed his hand from her mouth.

"Don't make any noise," he warned, seeing an empty bottle of laudanum on a nightstand beside her bed.

"I don't want to go," she protested feebly, as though she was in a trance.

"Sorry, miss, but I gave Bonnie my promise that I'd bring you back."

She looked at him strangely. "Do you know Bonnie LaRue?" she asked.

"She's one of my dearest friends. She asked me to see if I could bring you back to her and your parents."

"I need my medicine," she told him, turning to the nightstand. "Is that bottle empty?"

"I'm afraid it is, and right now you don't need anything to slow you down. I expect to have a difficult time getting you out of here."

"I won't leave without my medicine," she replied, closing her eyes. "I need it for my headaches."

"Right now, little lady, there isn't any choice. You've got to leave with me and not make any noise going down those stairs. I haven't got time to argue with you."

She looked at him then. "Carl will have you killed if you try to take me away. He has these men working for him who know how to shoot."

"I know a little bit about shooting," Slocum said as he took her by the arm.

"I'll scream," she told him, "and then Carl's men will stop you."

"I'm sure they're gonna try, Miss Dubois. But a thing like this isn't over until the last shot gets fired, and it makes a big difference who fires that shot. I'm asking you real nice one more time to come with me quietly."

"I won't do it," she said as he pulled her to a sitting position.

"Then you aren't giving me any choice," Slocum said.

He seized her by the hair, forcing her back against the pillow, dropping Younger's pistol on the mattress. As she opened her mouth to scream he covered it again, this time with one of the scarves.

He tied it behind her head as she struggled weakly to free herself from his grasp. In her drugged state she offered little resistance, although her fingernails scratched his shirt-sleeves while she began kicking the bedsheets off her legs.

"Lie still, Miss Dubois," he whispered, turning her over on her back to bind her wrists with the second scarf. As he tied the knots he glanced over to Younger, finding him still unconscious from the blow to his head.

"Now then," he said, gathering the struggling girl in his arms with the .44 in his right fist. "I'm gonna carry you down the stairs. Let's hope nobody's waiting for us when we get to the bottom, 'cause I sure as hell wouldn't want a bullet to hit you accidentally. If they're smart, they won't be shooting at you."

That seemed to make her relax. He carried her to the bedroom door and opened it a crack with his free hand, peering into the hallway.

"So far, so good," he said to himself, beginning a slow walk down the poorly lit hall.

At the top of the staircase he hesitated, gazing down at the foyer below. The house was quiet. Oil lamps on a wall near the coat tree gave off precious little light, not quite enough for him to be certain of what awaited him.

He started down the steps very slowly, aiming the pistol in front of him. Josephine lay quietly in his arms and for that, he was thankful.

A board creaked softly under his weight, making him pause just long enough to see if the sound caught anyone's attention. For several seconds, all was quiet.

He descended the staircase without incident, listening to the silence. "I wonder where everybody is," he whispered, unable to believe his good fortune. He was twenty or thirty feet from the front door and as of this moment, no shots had been fired at him.

At the bottom of the steps he cocked an ear toward James's study at the end of a dark hallway. No light was visible below the door. "I can't be this lucky," he said, taking a few short strides toward the front doorway with his head turned so he could see over his shoulder.

At just the wrong moment, Josephine began to squirm and make soft sounds, muffled by the scarf. She started kicking, fighting the cloth around her wrists.

"Be still," Slocum warned, worrying that even these quiet noises might be heard by someone in the house. "You'll get us both killed if you don't shut up."

She glared at him, her dark eyes burning with an inner fire in light from the oil lamps.

"I'm quite serious," he whispered, inching closer to the door. "If you make any noise, somebody's liable to start shooting, and that won't be good for either one of us."

She went limp in his arms again.

"That's my girl," he told her, reaching for the doorknob as his senses readied for what might await them outside. "Be real still and don't make sounds. That's the only way we've got any chance of getting out of here alive."

He found no one on the front porch guarding the door, and he supposed it was because the hour was late. He crept out on the porch, searching the darkness for a certain cypress tree where he'd left his weapons.

Slocum went down the porch steps two at a time, all the while expecting to hear a voice, a warning shout, or the bang of a gun. Thus far, luck was with him tonight, but experience had taught him never to count on Lady Luck— she would abandon him when he needed her most.

He carried the girl across a neatly trimmed front lawn in the dark, aiming for a row of cypress trees near the edge of the bayou surrounding the plantation.

"Just a few more yards," he said under his breath, as if

he were saying it to Josephine to keep her quiet.

Slocum was almost sure he'd spotted the right tree fork in spite of total darkness when he heard a sound behind him. A voice in the distance cried, "What the hell's goin' on?"

He hurried as fast as he could now, burdened with the girl in his arms, wondering how many ticks of the clock he would have in his favor before gunfire erupted. Down in his gut he knew it had all been too easy, getting Miss Dubois away from such a heavily armed place, and as the voice sounded he understood that his luck had probably just run out.

"Hey, Billy!" someone shouted. "That Slocum feller ain't in his room!"

"Where the hell's Clay?" another voice demanded.

Slocum made it to the trees at the edge of the swamp before he heard the same voice reply, "He's out cold in the woman's room with blood runnin' off his head!"

"Find that son of a bitch Slocum!" a third voice yelled.

"Hey, Billy! The woman's gone too!"

Slocum was panting, completely out of breath, when he found the fork in a tree where he'd hidden his shotgun and pistol. He put the girl down to retrieve his weapons with his pulse hammering in his ears. A shooting contest was about to begin, and he hoped he stood a chance of winning.

Glancing toward the house, he saw dark figures run out on the porch, outlined by white paint on the building's boards.

"Somebody run for the gates!" a distant voice cried. "He ain't got but one way out. Wake up Jack an' Cletus so they'll know to shoot the son of a bitch. But be careful you don't shoot the woman or Monsieur James will have your hide."

Slocum stuck Younger's .44 in the waistband of his pants

and pocketed his bellygun before he took the shotgun in his fist and bent down to pick up the girl again. He could hear soft curses from the night near the house, although for the moment he couldn't see anyone approaching.

"I'll have to wade this damn swamp," he said, turning into the forest. "Let's hope these alligators ain't all that hungry tonight."

He treaded lightly across marsh grasses and swampy ground in between stands of trees, listening to far-off voices sound yet another alarm close to the gates. Carrying the girl, he made slow progress across uncertain footing in an inky black forest, until he saw moonlight reflected off water just a few yards in front of them.

"This is where it gets tricky, little lady," he told Josephine quietly, coming to the edge of the swamp. "This place is plumb full of things that want to eat us, or give us a dose of poison. Be real still now."

He waded slowly into the bayou with the girl in his arms, trying to keep his shotgun high enough so it would remain out of the water while placing each foot carefully, at the same time keeping an eye out for alligators and snakes.

"This is sure as hell more than I bargained for," he said to himself, water creeping into his boots, as he searched for the right direction—too many things to do at once.

"Get some lanterns an' start lookin' for 'em!" a deep voice shouted in the distance. "Cover every goddamn inch of this place till you find 'em!"

Off to Slocum's right he heard a squeaking noise, and he remembered the sound and what Tomo had said about an alligator's warning when anything got too close. "I'd rather face fifty Apaches on the warpath than this," he muttered, each footfall less certain as water deepened around him.

Josephine struggled again, resisting her gag and the scarf around her wrists.

"Be still, girl," Slocum snapped, keeping a close eye on the watery marshlands he had to tread to reach the road. "You keep on kicking like that and we'll be alligator food."

A quiet splash off to his left halted him in mid-stride as he turned toward the sound. He was sure an alligator had just left its resting place, aiming for them, and silently he hoped it wasn't a man-eater.

He continued forward cautiously, wondering if a shotgun blast would turn a gator away. Pellets wouldn't pierce water more than a few inches before being deflected.

"You owe me, Bonnie," he said angrily, mad at himself for allowing a woman to put him where he was now. "All I have to do is live long enough to collect. . . ."

20

Two men poled the flat-bottom skiff through tangles of lily pads and hydrilla, while a third man held a lantern aloft at the front of the boat. Carl James stood on the starboard side with a rifle in his hands, searching the darkness and a small cirlce of light cast by the lantern.

"They will be headed for the road," James said, his jaws so tight he could hardly speak. "Pole that way, and be careful. I know he's armed. I told those men guarding the gate to start up the road looking for him."

"The son of a bitch took my gun," Clay Younger said, "or I'd have killed him."

"You are being paid to be careful," James replied sarcastically, scanning every opening in a cypress forest ahead of them as the boat sliced through black waters. "You came to me highly recommended, and now I discover you don't have the qualifications to hold this job."

"He tricked me," Younger complained, holding the lantern a bit higher. "An' he was damn sure quick. The rotten bastard got to me when my back was turned.''

James did not hide the impatience in his voice. ''You should not have turned your back on him. An explanation for what happened seems obvious.''

''He wasn't armed. I didn't see no reason to be so damn careful when he wasn't carryin' a gun.''

''It would appear Mr. Slocum is an opportunist. He took advantage of the opportunity you gave him.''

''I'm gonna kill him,'' Younger swore, touching a lump on the back of his head.

''First, we have to find him,'' James remarked after another sweeping glance across the bayou and its dark places where huge cypress trees thick with Spanish moss made the darkness almost impenetrable without a light source.

''Wish Joe Wales was here,'' a man wielding one of the poles said. ''I swear, he can see in the dark.''

''We'll find them,'' James promised. ''Mr. Slocum does not know these swamps. He won't know which direction to go. My only hope is that Josephine is not harmed. Before any of you fire a shot, make sure she is not in the way.''

''Maybe he'll run across a nest of gators,'' Younger said in a hopeful way.

''That would be the worst possible result,'' James told him. ''I want Josephine returned to me safe and sound.''

''He looked like a city dude,'' another boatman said with a glance at the pistol belted to his waist. ''He won't have no idea how to git through this shithole.''

''He'll head for the road,'' James assured everyone. ''He's too smart to wander off into the bayou. I suspect he already gave my plantation a good looking-over in daylight before he took the chance of coming here at night. Cletus and his partner will get him if he strikes the road, although if he's as smart as I think he is, he'll use Josephine as a shield, or a hostage. We won't let him leave under any circumstances, unless he threatens her life. If I'm any judge of character he won't care what happens to her . . . he'll be out to save his own skin if he sees he's cornered.''

Younger cleared his throat, casting the lantern's beam in all directions. ''He ain't as dumb as he looked, Boss. An' I ain't all that sure he's some dude from out West. He didn't act a bit scared when I swore I'd kill him if'n I got on his trail someplace.''

''It is quite obvious he's an experienced man in most situations,'' James replied. ''But he may not know bayou country, and if he doesn't, he'll most likely make a mistake. The swamps can be most unforgiving.''

''I figure he's meetin' up with that goddamn Creole,'' one of the boatmen said. ''That yeller bastard is liable to know all about swamps an' such.''

''Mr. Wales and Mr. Carson have already taken care of Tomo Suvante,'' James said with assurance. ''Mr. Wales has never failed me, which is more than I can say for the rest of you.''

''That ain't fair, Boss,'' Younger growled. ''Wales took his gun away from him, an' I figured he was harmless without havin' a weapon.''

''He didn't take his better judgment,'' James replied, ''nor did he take away his faster reflexes. You failed me, Mr. Younger, and it sorely disappoints me. At a later date we may have to discuss the future of your employment here. For now, let us see if we can rectify your mistake by finding Slocum and Josephine before any harm befalls her.''

Younger fisted a borrowed .44. ''I'll kill the sumbitch an' you can count on that,'' he said, raising the lantern.

''You had your chance,'' James muttered, following the circle of light with the muzzle of a .44-caliber Winchester. ''Some men hesitate, and in many cases hesitation can prove to be fatal. I think you're lucky to be alive. Mr. Slocum is clearly not who we thought he was."

"I figure he's a bounty hunter," the second boatman offered as he steered them around a cypress stump. "Somebody paid him a bunch of loot to come after your lady."

"He hasn't earned it yet," James said, watching an alligator's eyes gleam in the lantern light from a mound of grass in the bayou. "He hasn't gotten out of here alive yet, although I pray he doesn't cost me my darling Josephine in this foolish attempt to escape with her."

"Yonder's a big gator," a boatman warned.

"I see him quite clearly, Mr. Ross. Keep poling us toward the road. Mr. Slocum is obviously lost in this swamp, and if we beat him to the only road out of here, he'll be left to his own devices and the forbearance of Louisiana's native reptiles, which are not know for forgiving natures."

The steady croak of hundreds of bullfrogs prevented James from hearing much beyond the conversation being held in his boat, and for a time he was forced to rely on his eyes to locate Slocum and the girl. All around them, fireflies winked, but in the cypress forest no moonlight could penetrate moss-laden limbs, and only the lantern's pale glow allowed him to see what lay ahead.

"I heard somethin'," Younger said, lowering his voice, as he crouched down to aim the pistol in front of him.

James turned an ear toward the front of the boat. "What was it?"

"Can't tell for sure. Sounded like a splash."

"I figure it's only a gator leavin' the bank somewheres up yonder," Ross said.

"Pole us in that direction," James ordered. "Let's see what caused the gator to move."

Shadows danced before them as the boat floated between thick cypress and tall swamp grasses. Their flatboat moved slowly in shallow water, impeded by thick clumps of lily pads and hydrilla in narrow spots.

James kept his eyes glued to the outer edge of the circle of light.

"More to the left," Younger said, pointing with the barrel of his gun. "I heard it over there."

A deep cypress forest lay to the left of the boat, with no visible passageway for their craft.

"That's the road over yonder," Ross announced from the back of the boat. "I can see the outline of them trees growin' beside it."

"Take us over there," James ordered, feeling his palms grow clammy around the stock of his rifle. "Two of us can walk the road while the others continue east across the bayou."

"I'd just as soon stay in this here boat," Ross said with conviction. "A goddamn gator ain't as likely to git up the nerve to take a bite out of this big hunk of wood."

"Suit yourself," James replied. "Mr. Younger and I will take to the roadway with the lantern."

"But he'll see the light an' shoot at us," Younger objected quickly.

"That's what you're being paid for, Mr. Younger," James told him, "to shoot back when someone shoots at me."

The boatmen steered their craft to the banks where the road led to the plantation. Younger got out first, followed closely by James.

"Keep going that way," James told Ross and his partner with the pole. "Don't shoot if you find them. I intend to give Mr. Slocum every chance to surrender without harming Josephine. But if you do fire a shot, make absolutely certain you hit him and not the girl."

James struggled up a grassy embankment to the road,

standing back just enough to be out of the light cast by the lantern Clay Younger was holding.

"Walk slowly, Mr. Younger. Carry the lamp high."

Younger turned around, glaring at James. "You're usin' me for bait to draw his fire, ain't you? Well I goddamn sure ain't gonna do it. That Slocum ain't no greenhorn. He'll know that by shootin' me, there's one less gun after him."

James did not seem angry when he said, "Very well then, Mr. Younger. I have no further need for you if you aren't willing to follow my orders. Turn out the lamp wick and put it down."

Younger wore a puzzled expression as he twisted down the wick until the flame went out. "Then you're firin' me?" he asked while placing the lantern near his feet.

"In a manner of speaking," James replied softly.

The thunder of a rifle shot lifted Clay Younger off his feet when a bullet struck his rib cage, knocking him back into the swamp waters with a splash.

"What the hell was that?" a voice cried from the flat-boat.

In the darkness there was no one to see James smile. "An unfortunate accident. Mr. Younger tripped over a tree root and shot himself when he fell. Keep looking for Mr. Slocum and my darling Josephine. I'll send someone back to see to Mr. Younger's condition as soon as possible."

James walked away from the spot, ejecting a spent cartridge from the firing chamber of his Winchester. Only one thing truly mattered tonight, the return of his beloved Josephine. Any man in his employ who wasn't willing to give every ounce of effort he had to the same end was entirely useless.

He crept along the road in his nightshirt and trousers, not fully dressed due to the need to hurry when it was discovered Slocum had left the house with Josephine. He'd known all along there was something about John Slocum that didn't add up, but after the telegram from Denver stating Slocum was a proprietor of mining camp saloons, he'd let his guard down. Now he was paying for his mistake.

The monotonous drone of croaking bullfrogs began to infuriate him, since the noise prevented him from hearing slight sounds at any distance that might be a man wading through the swamp. A swarm of mosquitoes followed him, biting his face and hands and arms, yet he scarcely noticed them, all his attention focused on the road ahead, and the swamplands on either side.

He knew Cletus and another gate guard were somewhere on the same road behind him, and two more armed men were poling through the bayou, hemming Slocum in. Only now did he wonder idly if he should perhaps have waited to kill Clay Younger—Younger was one more gun standing between Slocum and escape.

"He was useless," James mumbled, "letting that bastard get the drop on him with his own pistol." Younger was supposedly a top gunhand in the state of Missouri. "He wasn't good enough to make it in Louisiana," James added, sweeping the barrel of his rifle back and forth as he moved farther along the road in total darkness.

Off to his right he caught a glimpse of the flatboat moving slowly among cypress trunks. "He won't get away," James promised himself. "He's on foot, probably carrying the girl. She takes so much laudanum she couldn't walk, much less wade through this swamp. She'll slow him down, and that's when we'll catch up to him."

He knew Slocum couldn't have much of a head start and was alone, now that Wales and Carson had disposed of Tomo Suvante. If there was one man in his employ who always got a job done and did it right, it was Joe Wales.

"I see somethin' over yonder!" a distant voice cried from the direction of the boat. "It's a man walkin' in water up to his ass, an' it appears he's carryin' somethin'."

"Don't shoot yet!" James called out. "Keep him in sight and we'll give him a chance to surrender peacefully!"

"I don't see a damn thing," another voice said, softer than the first.

"Right there between them trees!"

James felt his heart begin to labor. At last, they'd cornered Slocum.

The roar of a shotgun blast came from just ahead, accompanied by the wink of a muzzle flash. The sound echoed throughout the forest.

"My eyes!" a terrified voice screamed, followed by a soft splash near the flatboat.

"Jesus!" a voice James recognized as the gunman named Ross exclaimed. "The sumbitch just blowed Billy plumb outa the boat!"

James stopped and hunkered down, sighting in on the place where he'd seen the igniting gunpowder. "You bastard," James hissed as his hands tightened around his rifle, searching the night for a target . . . anything he could shoot at. Somehow, Slocum had been able to take Billy Atkins down at tremendous range with a shotgun, and that required significant shooting skill.

"This isn't over yet, Mr. Slocum," he whispered, edging forward again.

21

Slocum staggered out on the bank with the girl in his arms, his chest heaving while he gasped for air. Off to his left he saw the dim outline of a road, the road to freedom if only he could carry the woman further without collapsing from exhaustion. The boat was behind him, coming closer, and someone had fired a rifle shot down the road in the direction of the plantation, a shot that didn't make much sense because he and Josephine had been well out of range. He figured it had to be one of James's men getting nervous, shooting at shadows, anything that moved.

He forced one foot in front of another, his boots making a squishing sound as water leaked out. He'd made it through the swamp without encountering any alligators, but now he faced an unknown number of two-legged reptiles.

Every once in a while the girl would struggle and kick, but for the most part she lay limply in his arms, her head lolling back from the effects of laudanum, making it easier to carry her. But as they reached dry land, and a narrow roadbed with few places to hide, Slocum knew the risks were about to increase. He made the edge of the road and looked both ways, finding it too dark to be sure of anything.

Turning away from the plantation, he walked as rapidly as he could with a hundred-pound burden while keeping his shotgun ready for trouble, aiming in front of him. In widely scattered spots a bit of moonlight reached the roadway where limbs covered with moss were not so thick. Thus he was able to see a bit more than he might have otherwise, although he was still walking almost blindly toward the next group of shadows.

Constantly looking over his shoulder, he had covered a distance of three or four hundred yards when, suddenly, a sound in front of them stopped him cold.

"I see you made it most of the way," a harsh voice said to him. "Trouble is, you ain't made it past me yet."

He knew the voice belonged to Joe Wales. With the girl against his chest and his shotgun aimed ahead, he stood rock-still beside the road.

"I've got the girl," he said, judging how far away Wales was hiding—it was far too dark to see him. "A shot in the wrong place might kill her."

"I make a business out of puttin' bullets where they belong, Slocum."

"Nobody's that good in the dark, Wales. If you kill her, you'll answer to James for it."

"I'll take the chance, unless you put that goose gun down an' let the girl go before you throw your hands up."

Slocum glanced to his right where the bayou reached the edge of the roadbed, a distance of five or six yards. If he lunged that way he might escape Wales's first bullet. What he needed was to buy some time until he could find Wales in the darkness.

"I'll drop the shotgun and lay her down. No sense hurting an innocent girl."

"I figure you're also totin' a pistol under that coat, so drop it too."

"On one condition," Slocum answered. "If I drop both guns you'll show yourself instead of hiding behind a tree like some bushwhacker." He carried two pistols in the waistband of his pants, one belonging to Younger, the other his bellygun with very limited range. Wales wouldn't guess he had both of them. But a killer like Joe Wales was most likely to shoot the minute he put Josephine and the guns down. Slocum knew he would have to act fast to save his skin.

"You ain't in no position to be settin' conditions, but I ain't scared to show myself," Wales replied, "after you put her down an' toss them guns."

Slocum wondered how well Wales could see him, how his sight could be so much better in the dark. He dropped the shotgun at his feet and knelt down, placing the girl on a bed of grass. As he stood up he reached inside his suit coat and tossed his bellygun aside, tensing for the moment when Wales started shooting.

"You gotta be a dumb son of a bitch," Wales said, and now a shadow moved just ahead, the outline of a man on a horse, and in a tiny shaft of starlight Slocum saw the gleam of gun metal in Wales's hand and he knew Wales meant to kill him.

Slocum's fist went diving inside his coat for Younger's .44 as a gun exploded, a bullet whining past his ear close enough for him to feel its hot breath. An instant later, Slocum aimed and fired, feeling the Colt slam into his palm as a stabbing yellow flame spat from the muzzle.

Wales tumbled backward over the cantle of his saddle and his horse reared, pawing its forelegs, terrified by the pair of gunshots. Slocum knew he'd only winged Wales in the shoulder, his aim thrown off by haste.

Wales rolled off his horse's rump in a ball as the animal bolted away. The gunman landed on his back, grunting, still clutching his revolver. He sat up quickly as Slocum was taking careful aim for Wales's chest.

The pistol in Slocum's hand clicked on an empty cylinder or a damp cartridge ruined by his travels through the swamp, and now he was staring death in the face, holding a useless gun. His only hope lay in diving for the shotgun lying beside Josephine, and that would draw Wales's fire, risking her life.

He had whirled to make a leap for the swamp when the concussion of a shotgun blast erupted behind Wales. Slocum crouched down, wondering where the shot had come from and who'd fired it, as the body of Joe Wales twisted crazily in midair, turning like a child's spinning top. Arms outstretched, flinging his pistol into the bayou, Wales flopped on his side, legs kicking as a cry like that of a wounded mountain lion came from his throat. He rolled down the edge of the roadbed and landed in shallow water with a soggy splash.

Slocum grabbed his shotgun, squatting down as low as he could until he knew who'd fired the shot. Was it one of James's men who'd fired recklessly, hitting the wrong target? he wondered.

Then he saw a shadow move, and he immediately recognized the hairless skull in front of him.

"Don't be shootin' till I see he be dead," Tomo said. "Be more men comin' pretty quick, so get dis girl an' bring her to my hoss so's we can carry her."

Slocum came slowly to his feet. "You don't have to look," he told Tomo. "Nobody could survive that much buckshot."

Tomo ignored him, walking carefully to the edge of the swamp where Wales lay. "Jus' the same, I's gonna look," the Creole replied. "Maybeso shoot him again to be sure he don't get up."

"He won't be getting up," Slocum assured him, picking up his bellygun before he lifted the unconscious girl. "There's at least one more in a boat out there, and some coming up this road behind me." He walked over to Tomo with the girl in his arms.

Tomo was staring down at Wales. The gunman's pale eyes were open, sightless now, looking up at the night sky and limbs above his head. "He don't be breathin'," Tomo said softly.

"He was just a man, a hired killer who got himself killed because he forgot to look behind him. Let's get this girl on your horse before the others show up."

"Voodoo witch say bullet don't kill him," Tomo remembered.

"This time, she was wrong. That's real blood running out of his body."

Finally Tomo seemed satisfied, but just then Slocum heard footsteps running toward them from the direction of the mansion.

"Carry this girl," Slocum whispered. "I'll slow them down until you get her on your horse."

Tomo took Josephine and broke into a run as though she was as light as a feather, trotting into the darkness beneath trees lining the road.

Slocum swung around, knelt down, and brought his shotgun to his shoulder. "Don't come any closer!" he shouted. "Joe Wales is dead and we've got the girl! You get any closer and I'll blow you to pieces!"

The running footfalls stopped. For a moment there was quiet and nothing moved.

"It's a lie!" a voice cried out from the night. "Wales went to Baton Rouge to eliminate your hired assassin, Tomo Suvante."

Slocum knew the voice belonged to James. "He couldn't get it done, and now he's dead. Drop your guns and come have a look for yourself. He's lying here in the bayou next to the road, and if you or any of your men try to follow us, the same thing's gonna happen to you. Miss Dubois is going back to New Orleans with us and if anybody tries to stop us, they're going to a grave."

More silence, and Slocum grew impatient. "This is my last warning, James. There's at least two dead bodies floating in this swamp, and there'll be a hell of a lot more if you ignore my warning."

"You're lying," James replied, softer now.

"The proof's lying right here on the north side of the road if you care to take a look. But if you get near us on the way to New Orleans, I'm personally gonna come after you with a gun and fill you full of holes. Stay away from her, if you've got good sense, because if I have to come back here for any reason, you're as good as dead."

After Slocum delivered his speech he crept backward, still keeping an eye on the roadway.

"You arrogant bastard!" James shrieked. "You deceived me with your lies . . . with your treachery!"

Moving farther away, covering his retreat with the shotgun, he answered, "You deceived a young girl with promises and laudanum. You kept her a prisoner here. If you ever come near her again, I'll kill you."

The following silence lingered, giving Slocum the opportunity to turn and run for Tomo's horse. Enough time had been wasted with threats. He'd make good on his promise if Carl James ever showed his face around Josephine Dubois in the future.

•   •   •

Leading the chestnut, they entered Baton Rouge with the girl lying over Tomo's saddle.

"We'll take her to the hotel so a woman I know there can clean her up," Slocum said.

Tomo gave what might pass for a grin. "You be needin' a bit of cleanin' yourself."

"A bath, a bottle of brandy, and a good cigar is damn sure what I need," he agreed, holding Josephine on the horse as he walked beside her. "Tomorrow morning we'll hitch up the buggy and take her back home."

Tomo glanced over his shoulder. "You don't be thinkin' Monsieur James come try us again?"

"Nope. Ain't likely. Some men have sense enough to know when they can't win. I think Carl James learned a lesson tonight about money and guns."

"Maybeso we should go back an' kill him," Tomo suggested in a darkly serious way.

"I don't believe any further measures are necessary," Slocum said as they turned down a dark street toward the hotel. He had to guess at the hour, probably three or four in the morning, and now, as things appeared settled, he felt almost too tired to go the rest of the way.

As they entered the Grand Lenier, a sleepy-eyed clerk got up from a chair behind the desk. He took one look at Slocum's filthy clothing, then another directed toward the unconscious girl in his arms, and lastly at Tomo.

"We don't allow no nigras in here," the old man said.

Slocum headed for the stairs. "You'll allow this one in tonight," he said coldly. "Send Miss Claudette up to the bath with buckets of hot water and clean towels."

"But we don't allow—"

Slocum halted midway up the steps. "Shut up, and send the girl upstairs with water like I told you," he snapped.

"I'd hate like hell to have to put this woman down long enough to rearrange the shape of your face, but I damn sure will unless you do what I say. I've had enough Louisiana bullshit for one night."

"Yessir, Mr. Slocum," the clerk replied, coming out from behind his counter to fetch Claudette. "It may take a spell for her to heat the water. It ain't the usual time for folks to be askin' for a bath."

"And send up two bottles of brandy and a handful of cigars, the best you've got," Slocum added, resuming his climb toward the second floor. "I don't give a damn what it costs."

"Everythin' will be right up quick as I can get Claudette to stoke the stove," he said, hurrying down a hallway to the back.

He handed Tomo the girl gently and took his room key from his water-soaked pocket, feeling fatigue wash over him like a tidal wave. "Put her on the bed till the girl comes up with hot water," he instructed Tomo.

"She ain't woke up hardly at all," Tomo observed as he took her into Slocum's room.

"It's the laudanum. When it wears off she'll be okay. In the meantime, go put your horse in the livery around back and come back here. We've got some brandy to drink, and cigars to smoke. It's been one hell of a long night."

Tomo rested Josephine on the mattress. As he was leaving the room he spoke. "I got somethin' to say, Mr. Slocum. I had you figured wrong. Didn't think you knowed how to take care of yourself. You showed me different."

Slocum slumped into a chair at the foot of the bed. "You handled yourself right well," he said. "Some men just have a knack for it, no matter what part of the country they come from. I imagine you'd handle yourself right well fighting Apaches, or just about anybody. Now, go put that horse away and we'll start some serious drinking.''

Tomo grinned and hurried out of the room.

22

Bonnie's eyes were shining, and he couldn't be sure if it was the result of happy tears, or reflected light from crystal lamps suspended from the ceiling. She held Slocum close, looking up into his face while Marcel Dubois embraced his daughter, crying openly, as was Josephine's mother. Their joyous reunion was the result of a telegram Slocum had sent to New Orleans ahead of him to announce the time of his arrival with Josephine. Josephine's parents were waiting for them at Bonnie's when they drove up just before the hour struck ten on Friday night.

"You'll have to tell me all about it later," Bonnie said, glancing over her shoulder, smiling when she saw the family together in her anteroom.

"The girl's had a rough couple of days recovering from the laudanum," Slocum said. "She was better this morning. She says she doesn't remember much of what happened. Her memories of it are pretty hazy."

"Perhaps it's for the best," Bonnie whispered, snuggling

against Slocum's neck. "I'm sure it wasn't easy, getting her away from that bastard Carl James."

Slocum aimed a thumb over his shoulder. Tomo was behind him slouched against a door frame leading into the hall. "Your Creole friend deserves most of the credit. He knew that country like the back of his hand, and that's the reason me and the girl didn't wind up in some alligator's belly."

Bonnie acknowledged Tomo with a smile and a nod. "Most of my friends warned me not to trust him, in the beginning. But I had faith in him. I'm a pretty good judge of character, as you already know."

"He did his share of the killing too," Slocum told her in a quiet voice, so the girl and her family couldn't hear. "James had himself surrounded by some mighty tough customers, but wasn't any of 'em any tougher than Tomo."

"Did you kill him?"

"If you mean Carl James, the answer is no. We had to do away with most of his hired guns."

"You're talking about Clay Younger, aren't you."

"That's the funny thing," Slocum remembered. "The next day as we were heading out for New Orleans, someone Tomo knew told him that Younger was dead, only I didn't kill him and neither did Tomo, so it's hard to figure how he died. Don't reckon it matters all that much. Tomo downed the worst of 'em, a shooter by the name of Joe Wales, and in the process he saved my hide and most likely saved the girl. Right at the last we had to shoot our way out of there."

"I wish you'd gotten rid of James," she said. "Now I fear he'll come back for Josephine."

"I'd nearly stake my life he won't. He got a taste of the lead Tomo throws around, and I warned James that if he came near the girl again, I'd come back here and kill him. He don't strike me as being stupid. I doubt you'll ever hear from him again. He lost face in the eyes of too many people up there, what with dead men who worked for him floating all over the swamp. He'll swing wide of you and Josephine from now on. He won't care to tangle with Tomo again, and I don't figure he wants any more of me either.''

Marcel Dubois came over to Slocum and Bonnie, wiping tears from his eyes. "Just name your price, Mr. Slocum. What you have given us back is worth everything I have, and more.''

"There's no charge, Mr. Dubois,'' Slocum replied. "We had some expenses, not much, and you can pay those if you want. I did it because a dear friend asked me for help, not for money.''

"But I'll gladly pay whatever you ask.''

Slocum shook his head. "This isn't about money. It's about something far more valuable, a friendship I can count on when I need it.''

"I'll leave a few hundred dollars with Miss LaRue,'' Marcel said, "for the expenses. We're taking Josephine home now. She hasn't eaten well and has lost a great deal of weight. The first thing my wife intends to do is feed her.''

Josephine, with her long black hair tied back, came over to Slocum and kissed his cheek. "Thank you so very much for what you did, Mr. Slocum. I'm sorry I was such a bother right at first.''

"No bother,'' he said. "Your thanks should go to Tomo. I couldn't have done it without him. He did most of the work.''

Josephine walked over to Tomo and kissed him. "Thank you, Mr. Suvante. I hope you won't mind my saying so, but for a big man with such a frightening appearance, you can be the gentlest person. Thank you for saving me.''

Tomo nodded his silent acceptance of her gratitude, and took a step back to allow Josephine and her parents to leave the room arm in arm.

Bonnie spoke to Slocum when Honey, the girl he'd met when he'd first arrived, showed the Dubois family to the front door.

"How much do I really owe you, John?" she asked. "I would never have asked you to come all this way out of your own pocket to handle a matter that was none of your affair."

He thought about it a moment. "Instead of money, I saw this object upstairs in your bedroom before we left for Baton Rouge, and I'd like to look at it again."

"An object. What object?" Bonnie's brow furrowed.

"I'll show you," he replied, taking her by the arm. "It was creamy white and soft, the best I remember, and this object had long blond hair done up in curls. Biggest breasts I ever saw too, and if you don't mind, I'd like to lie down in bed next to that same object again."

She froze at the bottom of a staircase leading to the second-floor bedrooms. She gave him a mock scowl. "Are you saying I'm some sort of object, Mr. Slocum? Is that how you feel about all women?"

"Nope," he replied, hiding the beginnings of a grin. "I simply didn't know what else to call something so beautiful. I ran out of words. Now get up those stairs, because I haven't run out of something else I'd like to show you, something of my own."

She giggled and touched his cheek with her fingertips. "It didn't take you long to make up your mind what you wanted. As to the . . . object you want to show me, would you believe me if I told you I've been dreaming about it every night since you left?''

''All women are liars,'' he told her, kissing her lips gently before he guided her up the stairs.

A special offer for people who enjoy reading the
best Westerns published today.

If you enjoyed this book, subscribe now and get...

TWO FREE WESTERNS

A $7.00 VALUE–NO OBLIGATION

If you would like to read more of the very best, most exciting, adventurous, action-packed Westerns being published today, you'll want to subscribe to True Value's Western Home Subscription Service.

TWO FREE BOOKS

When you subscribe, we'll send you your first month's shipment of the newest and best 6 Westerns for you to preview. With your first shipment, two of these books will be yours as our introductory gift to you absolutely *FREE* (a $7.00 value), regardless of what you decide to do.

Special Subscriber Savings

When you become a True Value subscriber you'll save money several ways. First, all regular monthly selections will be billed at the low subscriber price of just $2.75 each. That's at least a savings of $4.50 each month below the publishers price. Second, there is never any shipping, handling or other hidden charges— *Free home delivery*. What's more there is no minimum number of books you must buy, you may return any selection for full credit and you can cancel your subscription at any time. A TRUE VALUE!

Mail the coupon below

To start your subscription and receive 2 FREE WESTERNS, fill out the coupon below and mail it today. We'll send your first shipment which includes 2 FREE BOOKS as soon as we receive it.